Blue Ribbon Summer

Don't Miss

MARGUERITE HENRY'S

Ponies *of* Chincoteague

Book 1: *Maddie's Dream*

Coming Soon

Book 3: *Chasing Gold*

CATHERINE HAPKA

Aladdin
New York London Toronto Sydney New Delhi

ALADDIN
An imprint of Simon & Schuster Children's Publishing Division
1230 Avenue of the Americas, New York, NY 10020
This Aladdin paperback edition July 2014

Also available in an Aladdin hardcover edition.
For information about special discounts for bulk purchases, please contact Simon & Schuster Special Sales at 1-866-506-1949 or business@simonandschuster.com.
The Simon & Schuster Speakers Bureau can bring authors to your live event. For more information or to book an event contact the Simon & Schuster Speakers Bureau at 1-866-248-3049 or visit our website at www.simonspeakers.com.
Book design by Karina Granda
The text of this book was set in Adobe Caslon Pro.
Manufactured in the United States of America 0514 OFF
2 4 6 8 10 9 7 5 3 1
Library of Congress Control Number 2014936333
ISBN 978-1-4814-0340-5 (hc)
ISBN 978-1-4814-0339-9 (pbk)
ISBN 978-1-4814-0341-2 (eBook)

Blue Ribbon Summer

◆ CHAPTER ◆
1

BROOKE RHODES YAWNED AND POKED HER glasses farther up her nose as she walked across her backyard. It was early, probably not even seven thirty, though Brooke wasn't sure, since she'd forgotten to put on her watch. Already, though, the heat made her feel lazy and sluggish, as if she should kick off her sneakers and cool her feet in the dew-damp grass.

There was a muffled thump from inside the small barn at the back of the tidy patch of lawn. Swallowing another yawn, Brooke hurried forward and shoved at the barn door. It resisted, remaining stubbornly shut. The humidity, Brooke's stepfather said. He'd promised all last summer to sand down the door so it worked better, but the chore had never quite made it to the top of his to-do list. Brooke wasn't holding her breath for this summer either.

Another thump came from inside the barn, followed by a surprisingly deep nicker. Brooke smiled.

"Relax, Foxy girl. I'm coming," she called.

She shoved harder and the door finally gave way, letting Brooke into the tiny barn. Well, Brooke liked to call it a barn, anyway. The Amish builders who'd come from St. Mary's County to put it up had referred to it as a shed. It was a long, low wooden structure with a corrugated metal roof. Half of it was enclosed into a combination feed, tack, and general storage room, while the other half was an open stall where Foxy could come in out of the rain, heat, or wind, and where her food and water buckets hung. Brooke liked to call the two sections the pony part and the people part.

Foxy was staring over the Dutch door between the two halves, ears pricked, when Brooke let herself into the people part of the barn. "Don't worry, breakfast is coming," Brooke said, reaching out to rub the pony's nose as she hurried past. "Just hang on. . . ."

She grabbed her battered old feed scoop and opened the metal trash can in the corner that held Foxy's grain. The scoop had been a gift from the neighbors when Foxy had first come home four years earlier, and Brooke wouldn't have replaced it with a newer or fancier one even if she could afford to, because it reminded her of that day—one of the best of her life. She scooped out the proper amount of feed in one expert movement and headed for the Dutch door.

"Out of the way, Foxy." Brooke poked the pony in the chest, and Foxy moved aside as Brooke let herself into the stall area. After dumping the feed into Foxy's pink plastic bucket, Brooke stepped back to allow the mare to dive in.

Brooke stood with Foxy for a moment, a hand on the pony's glossy chestnut shoulder. This was always one of her favorite times of the day. It was even better now that school was out and Brooke didn't have to rush off to meet the bus.

"What should we do today, girl?" Brooke murmured, picking absently at a spot of dried mud on the pony's coat. "Maybe go for a ride before it gets too hot?"

Foxy flicked an ear her way, though she didn't lift her

head from the bucket. Brooke's gaze wandered out the open front of the shed. The sun was already burning the last of the dew off the grass. On the far side of Foxy's three-acre pasture, Brooke saw that the neighbors' retired draft horses had already taken up residence under the big oak tree on the property line, dozing and flicking their tails against the flies. It was going to be a hot one. Maybe it would be better to wait and ride after dinner.

A few minutes later Brooke let herself into the house through the back door. The kitchen smelled like coffee and toast. On the TV tucked under the cherrywood cabinets, a local newscaster was blabbering about the traffic. At the table, Brooke's five-year-old twin brother and sister were chattering at each other, though Brooke couldn't hear what they were saying over the sound of her stepfather's booming voice. He was standing at the counter, his cell phone pressed to his ear with one hand while he fiddled with the coffee maker with the other.

Stepping over to the toaster, Brooke grabbed the bread someone had left nearby. Her mother glanced at her.

"Oh, sweetie," she said. "There you are. What's on

your agenda for today? Are you okay staying by yourself for a while? I've got an open house in . . ." She glanced at her gold watch and her eyes widened. "Less than forty minutes. I've got to go!"

At that moment Brooke's stepfather hung up the phone. "I'm off," he told his wife, stepping over to give her a peck on the cheek. "Got a hot lead on someone looking for a classic Corvette, and they want to come in right now."

"Can you drop the twins off at day camp on your way to the lot?" Brooke's mother asked. "I'm running late."

"Sure." Brooke's stepfather ruffled Ethan's hair. "Come on, twins. First one to the garage gets to ride shotgun."

Brooke's mother rolled her eyes. "No shotgun! I keep telling you, Roger, they're too young. Backseat only, you two. In your car seats, straps buckled." She bustled over to the table, efficiently packing Ethan and Emma into their Velcro sandals and sun hats.

Brooke's stepfather grabbed his keys. "Need me to drop you off anywhere, Brooke?" he asked.

"No thanks." Brooke shrugged. "I was just going to hang around here today. Maybe go for a ride or something."

"Good, good." Brooke could tell her stepfather wasn't really listening. He had his cell phone out again, scrolling through the messages.

Moments later the others were gone and Brooke had the house to herself. She wandered over to switch off the TV, waving a hand to shoo away the flies buzzing over the crumbs the twins had left everywhere. Why did it sometimes feel as if her family forgot she was even around?

She shrugged off the thought. Her family was busy, that was all. Her stepfather's used car lot was the most successful one on the Eastern Shore of Maryland. *Let Rhodes put you on the road*—that was his slogan, and everyone Brooke met seemed to know it. Sometimes she wished she still had her old last name, Bradley. But when Brooke was six years old, her stepfather had officially adopted her, and her mother had insisted they all have the same last name, saying that would help make them a family. Brooke didn't really mind, especially since her real father had died when she was too young to remember him. But she sometimes wished she'd at least been given a choice.

That was how Brooke's mother did things, though.

When she made a decision, she stuck to it: no second thoughts. She was the type of person who couldn't stay still for more than two minutes at a time unless she was asleep. She'd gone back to selling real estate the moment the twins started preschool, and when she wasn't at the office or visiting a sale property, she was tidying her own house or shopping or doing any of the zillion other things she did every day.

Brooke got tired just thinking about it. She definitely hadn't inherited her mom's energy level or need to be involved in everything. In fact, she loved nothing more than spending an entire afternoon lying in the grass watching Foxy graze, or curling up for hours to read a book, whether it was a horse care or training manual or her very favorite classic story, *Misty of Chincoteague*. Brooke had read the story of the Beebe children and their special pony so many times that every page was dog-eared and the cover was starting to come loose.

The ding of the toaster broke Brooke out of her thoughts. Grabbing her toast, she tossed it onto a plate, then poured herself a glass of orange juice. Wandering into the den, she set her breakfast down next to the computer. The screen was a lot bigger than the one on her laptop, and she was hoping Maddie had put more photos on the Pony Post.

The Pony Post was a private online message board with just four members. Brooke had never met the other three in person, but she considered them among her best friends. Over the past year and a half, the four of them had bonded over their shared love of Chincoteague ponies.

Maddie Martinez had been the one to come up with the idea of the site. She lived in northern California and rode a Chincoteague mare named Cloudy who was the spitting image of the original Misty. Maddie was the type of person Brooke wished she could be—active, outgoing, and fun-loving.

Then there was Nina Peralt. She lived in New Orleans with her parents and owned a pony named Bay Breeze. She was one of the coolest people Brooke knew—sociable and artsy and smart—and her whole big-city existence seemed very sophisticated compared to Brooke's life.

The final member was Haley Duncan, who lived on a small farm in Wisconsin. Her pony was a spunky gelding named Wings that Haley leased from a neighbor. Haley was bold and determined and focused, which were all traits that Brooke guessed were very necessary for Haley's chosen sport of eventing.

Sometimes Brooke's friend Adam made fun of her "imaginary friends," as he called them. But Brooke couldn't imagine life without Maddie, Nina, Haley, and the Pony Post.

Brooke chewed a bite of toast as she logged on to the Internet. Soon the familiar Pony Post logo popped up. It showed four Chincoteague ponies galloping through the surf on Assateague Island, which was only an hour or so down the coast from where Brooke was sitting at that very moment.

Quite a few new posts had appeared since Brooke had checked in the evening before. There were several new photos, too, just as she'd hoped. Maddie had participated in a special trail ride at her barn the previous weekend, and she'd been sharing photos ever since.

[MADDIE] Check it out, guys—my friends e-mailed me more pix from the Snack &

Swim. Vic even got one of me diving off

Cloudy's back! Hope you like them!

[NINA] Fab photos! Wish we could do something like that at my barn. But I guess we'd have to swim in the Mississippi River, lol! Probably not such a brilliant idea.

[HALEY] LOL! Def. not. We don't want u and Breezy to get swept out into the Gulf of Mexico!

[NINA] No worries, we already know all our ponies can swim, right?

Brooke smiled as she read her friends' comments. Their ponies' special heritage was what had originally drawn the Pony Post members together. But only Brooke had actually seen her pony swim across the channel between Assateague and Chincoteague islands during the annual pony penning. That was almost four years ago, when

Brooke was barely eight years old, but she remembered it as if it had happened yesterday.

Brooke had loved horses and ponies for as long as she could remember. She'd started riding at age five on the neighbors' gentle, patient draft horses, and had taken weekly riding lessons the summer she was seven, though somehow there hadn't seemed to be enough time or money to continue after the twins came along. Brooke had dreamed of her own pony for so long that when her parents had finally agreed to let her use her saved-up allowance and birthday money to buy one at the Chincoteague pony auction, Brooke had barely dared to believe it.

Actually, Foxy hadn't been her first choice. Brooke had hoped to find a pinto like the famous Misty. She'd stayed at the pony pens long after her parents had lost interest and wandered off to find something to eat, looking over each spindly-legged foal and taking notes to help herself remember which were her favorites. She'd spotted a sweet-faced bay filly with markings similar to Misty's, and a little buckskin colt with bold white splashes on both sides. Those had been her favorites, though Brooke had also picked out two or three other cute spotted foals.

Then the pony auction had started. When the bay filly's turn came, Brooke never even got the chance to bid. The opening bid was double the total amount she had to spend. Within seconds, other bidders had jumped in, and Brooke didn't even hear the final price.

"Never mind, sweetie," her mother had said. "You can try for the next one."

But the buckskin colt had sold for triple Brooke's top price, and the others for more than that. Even the solid-colored foals were more expensive than she could afford.

Finally there were only a few young ponies left. One of them was a gangly yearling filly that Brooke had barely noticed in the pens, a chestnut with a lighter mane and tail. She didn't fit Brooke's idea of the perfect Chincoteague pony. But she had a soft eye and a calm temperament, and at that moment, that had been enough for Brooke to raise her hand when the auctioneer called for bids. Brooke had never regretted ending up with Foxy—or forgotten the way her stepfather had kicked in an extra hundred dollars at the last minute so Brooke could buy her.

Brooke smiled as she thought back to that exciting day, even as she continued to scan the rest of the new entries on the Pony Post.

[NINA] What are you and Cloudy up to now that the Snack & Swim is over? And how about the rest of you? Haley, Brooke?

[MADDIE] Back to reg. lessons. Ms. Emerson says we're going to start doing some jumping gymnastics. Should be fun! I love jumping, and so does Cloudy!!

[NINA] Cool! I just started doing more jumping too, mostly b/c I found out my barn is having a show this fall. There's going to be a costume class too! Can't wait to think of ideas for that!!

[HALEY] Excellent! What other classes will u enter?

[NINA] Not sure yet—my instructor says we'll figure it out by the end of the summer. What about u, Haley? Got any events coming up or anything?

[HALEY] Wings and I have big plans for this summer. I have almost enough $ saved up for another lesson w/ my XC coach.

[MADDIE] XC? That's cross-country, right? Like jumping over big giant logs and other scary stuff like that?

[HALEY] LOL! It's not that scary—it's fun! U should try it sometime . . .

Brooke scanned the rest of the entries. Nina and Maddie asked Haley more questions about eventing, then added more about their own lessons. They all had such big plans for themselves and their ponies for the summer!

And what plans do I have? Brooke wondered, nibbling

at her toast, which had gone cold as she read. Nothing. Just riding around the neighborhood trying not to get sunburned or eaten alive by mosquitoes and blackflies. Big whoop.

She sighed. It wasn't as if she had much choice. Lessons and shows cost money, and Brooke never seemed to have enough of that. She'd recently spent everything she'd saved up from her allowance and the past couple months of odd jobs—washing cars at the lot, feeding the neighbors' drafts when they went out of town, the occasional babysitting gig—on fly spray and horse treats, a new hoofpick to replace the one she'd lost somehow and a new halter to replace the one Foxy had broken. There never seemed to be an end to the expenses a pony could run up!

Still, Brooke knew she should stop feeling sorry for herself. She was lucky to have a pony at all. She was lucky her parents had helped her buy Foxy, and that they paid for the pony's basic needs, even if her stepfather still grumbled every time he swiped his credit card at the feed store or wrote a check to the farrier who trimmed Foxy's hooves.

She skimmed her friends' posts again. Their summer

plans sounded so exciting. But why should they have all the fun? Even if Brooke and Foxy wouldn't be showing—or even taking lessons—anytime soon, that didn't mean they couldn't train as if they were. Right?

Brooke's mood brightened as she turned the idea over in her head. She owned a whole shelf full of books about horses and riding, and there were more in the library, not to mention plenty of videos online. She'd done most of Foxy's training herself so far, with lots of research and advice from her neighbors and others. And Foxy was five now—old enough to do anything Brooke wanted to do with her. So why not get more serious about their training? It would be fun!

"Thanks, guys," Brooke murmured, closing the Pony Post page. She'd wait and update her friends later. Right now she was eager to head back out to the barn and get started on her own big plans.

Brooke dropped her dishes in the sink, then went back outside. It was hotter already, and the drone of insects filled the air. Brooke grabbed Foxy's halter as she entered through the people part of the barn, then headed out into the pasture. Foxy was grazing in her favorite spot right across the fence from the draft horses' shade tree. She lifted her head when Brooke called her, then ambled over to meet her owner.

"Hey, girl," Brooke whispered, running her hand up the pony's sleek reddish-brown neck to scratch her favorite spot. "Ready to become a show horse?"

Foxy curled her neck, her lower lip flopping with pleasure as she leaned into the scratch. After a moment Brooke slid the halter onto Foxy's head, then led her over to the hitching ring in the run-in stall.

"Be right back," Brooke said, giving the mare a pat. She hurried back into the people part of the barn. She kept her grooming tools in a bucket that had held Foxy's water for the first few months Brooke had owned her. That winter, the bucket had cracked in the first hard freeze, and Brooke had had to beg her parents for the money to replace it with a rubber one. But the plastic one still worked fine to hold her grooming stuff.

Soon she was hard at work brushing the dirt out of Foxy's coat and picking burrs and twigs out of her mane and tail. By the time the mare was halfway clean, Brooke was sweaty and panting as if she'd just run halfway to Salisbury. The thought of lugging her saddle out of the barn and tacking up made her want to lie down and take a nap in the shade.

"Maybe it's too hot to start our training right now," she told Foxy, who had one hind foot cocked and appeared to be half asleep. Brooke glanced down at herself, realizing something else. "Besides, I forgot to change clothes."

She'd ridden countless times in her current outfit of shorts and tennis shoes, but rarely in a saddle. The leathers of her English saddle always pinched her bare legs, and the fenders on her battered old Western one rubbed.

Brooke hesitated, glancing toward the house. It wouldn't take long to run inside and change into jeans and paddock boots. But was it really worth it on such a hot day?

Instead, she ducked into the people part just long enough to grab her plastic schooling helmet and Foxy's bridle. Moments later, she was slipping on to Foxy bareback from the fence rail. She glanced at the humble riding ring she'd laid out in one corner of the pasture, then tugged on one rein to turn Foxy in the other direction.

"It's no big deal," she murmured, rubbing the mare's withers as they set out along the edge of the soybean field next door. "We can start our training tomorrow."

◆ CHAPTER ◆ 2

BROOKE HAD STARTED OUT WITH NO particular destination in mind. But it wasn't long before she realized she was almost automatically heading toward Adam's house.

Adam Conley was the only other kid Brooke's age within a five-mile radius. The two of them had been hanging out since they were toddlers, and they usually spent most of the summer bombing around together, exploring their rural little corner of the county, Brooke on Foxy and Adam on his souped-up dirt bike.

This year was different, though. Brooke couldn't remember the last time Adam had showed up at the screen door during breakfast, already bored and looking for something to do. In fact, she'd barely seen him since school had let out almost a month earlier.

It's only because he's on the swim team this year, Brooke told herself, squeezing with both legs to hold herself in place as Foxy picked her way down one of the few hills in their mostly pancake-flat area.

But was that really all it was? Brooke couldn't help remembering that Adam hadn't hung out with her much during the last few months of school, either. He'd seemed more interested in spending time with other boys—playing basketball with them after school, goofing off with them at lunch, elbowing them as they all loped down the halls together between classes. And mostly ignoring Brooke, barely nodding when she said hi and never coming over to talk during homeroom. Brooke hadn't been sure what to do about that, so she hadn't done anything. But it hurt a little to think maybe he didn't like her as much anymore.

Still, it wasn't as if she didn't have any other friends. She'd had plenty of people to sit with at lunch or pair up with for school projects. But none of those girls lived close by, and none of them had called or even texted much so far that summer.

“Whatever,” Brooke muttered aloud, not wanting to think about that anymore. She was sure Adam hadn’t really changed. They were older now, and busier, and it made sense that they couldn’t spend every second of the day hanging out the way they had when they were little kids.

For instance, Brooke’s new training plans would probably keep her just as busy as swim team practices and stuff were keeping Adam. Reading her friends’ posts had given her lots of ideas, and suddenly she wished she’d stayed home to get started after all.

Then she remembered something her old riding teacher had said once—that anytime you rode or handled a horse, you were always either training or untraining her. That had made a big impression on Brooke at the time, though she’d sort of forgotten about it lately.

Now the idea inspired her anew. She sat up straighter on Foxy’s back, shortening her reins, which she’d let slip out to the buckle. Foxy stopped, obviously thinking that was what her rider wanted.

"No, it's okay, girl. Walk on." Brooke clucked and nudged the pony's sides with her heels. Foxy shook her head against the snug reins, stepping awkwardly sideways.

Fine. If Foxy wanted to go sideways, maybe it was time to teach her to leg-yield better. Brooke had played around with teaching the mare a few moves like that after checking a book on dressage out of the library, though that had been during the winter, when the footing in their backyard ring wasn't very good, so they hadn't done much. Now Brooke tried to remember what the book had said.

"Outside leg on, bend to the inside—or was it to the outside?" Brooke couldn't remember. She bit her lip, then shrugged and just gave a kick with her right leg.

Instead of moving to the left, Foxy halted again. She lifted her head and backed up a step.

"No, Foxy," Brooke said. "You're supposed to be leg-yielding."

She nudged the mare forward again and gave it another try. This time Foxy kept walking, but actually veered to the right instead of the left when Brooke gave the leg aid for the leg-yield!

Oh well, Brooke thought. *Maybe I need to look at that dressage book again. Or maybe I'll look up some tips on the Internet later.*

She was almost to Adam's house anyway, so she gave up on training for the moment, instead pushing Foxy into a trot to get there faster.

Adam was in his front yard, kicking a half-deflated soccer ball back and forth between his bare feet. He glanced up when he heard Foxy coming.

"Hi!" Brooke called, holding the reins in one hand as she pushed up her glasses, which had slipped down her nose as they always did when it was hot.

"What are you doing here?" Adam asked.

Brooke shrugged. "Nothing. Just bored. Want to ride down to the creek or something?"

"I can't." Adam shot a look toward the quiet country road, which was deserted except for a crow pecking at a leaf. "I've got swim team. Justin will be here to pick me up soon, so . . ."

His voice trailed off, and he didn't quite meet Brooke's eye. Brooke knew him well enough to guess what he *wasn't* saying—he wanted her to scram before his ride arrived, probably because Justin was a year older and one of the most popular boys at school.

Before she could figure out how to feel about that, there was the sudden loud pop of a car backfiring at the end of the road. A second later a souped-up vintage Mustang peeled around the corner and sped toward them, engine roaring. Brooke knew the car—her stepdad had sold it to Justin's older brother, who was in high school.

The crow flew up with a squawk, and Foxy snorted and jumped to the side as the car screeched to a stop at the curb. "Easy, girl," Brooke murmured, grabbing a chunk of mane just in time to stop herself from sliding off the pony's back. How embarrassing would that be?

Justin jumped out of the passenger seat. "Yo, Conley!" he yelled. He did a double take as he noticed Brooke and Foxy standing there. "Whoa, a horse! Weird."

Adam laughed. "Yeah, that's just Brooke. She's, like, the neighborhood horse freak. Come on, let's jet."

Justin's brother revved the engine as Adam and Justin climbed into the car. Adam's door had barely shut behind him when the Mustang shot off again, tires squealing as it rounded the next bend in the road.

Foxy relaxed as soon as the car was out of earshot, though Brooke still felt tense. What had gotten into Adam lately? He'd always been her best friend—almost like a brother. But he wasn't acting like much of a friend lately. . . .

She shook her head, banishing those thoughts. What was the point in worrying about it? There was nothing she could do.

"At least I still have you, girl," she whispered, rubbing Foxy's neck. "Come on, let's take a nice long ride along the creek—just the two of us."

By five o'clock that afternoon it was hotter than ever. After her morning ride, Brooke had spent the next few hours in the air-conditioned house, looking through her shelf of horse books for training ideas. Only the need to feed Foxy had forced her to drag herself back outside.

Foxy was halfway through her grain and Brooke was outside the shed, topping off the mare's water tub with the hose, when she heard her stepfather calling her name from the direction of the house.

"He's home early today," she commented to Foxy. When her name drifted across the yard again, Brooke turned off the hose and shoved it back under the fence where Foxy couldn't reach it. The mare was still young, and had been known to play with things when the mood struck her. Those things often ended up damaged or destroyed as a result. That was what had happened to Foxy's last fly mask, and also to a couple of grooming brushes Brooke had left within the mare's reach. Brooke was already broke and definitely didn't want to spend the next two weeks scrubbing upholstery at the used car lot to pay for a new hose.

She hurried back to the house. Her stepfather was pacing back and forth in the kitchen. The twins were sitting at the table, paying no attention to their father or anything else as they argued loudly over the last cookie in the box.

"Ah, Brooke." Her stepfather stopped pacing and smiled at her. "There you are. Tammy!" he shouted. "Hurry up!"

"Coming, coming." Brooke's mother hurried in, her

high heels click-clacking on the linoleum. She was still all dressed up in her Realtor outfit of blazer, skirt, and panty-hose. Brooke didn't know how she stood it in this heat.

"What's happening, Daddy?" Ethan asked, looking away from the cookie just long enough for Emma to grab it and shove the entire thing into her mouth. "Hey!" Ethan yelped when he noticed.

"Never mind the cookie, honeybun. I'll take you out for ice cream after dinner if you want." Brooke's stepfather was obviously in a good mood. He grinned as Ethan cheered. Emma let out a whoop too, clearly assuming she was included in the ice cream offer.

"What's going on, Roger?" Brooke's mother sounded slightly impatient. "I'm right in the middle of updating the website, and—"

"I'm trying to tell you, okay?" he said. "Listen, you all know it's been a pretty great month at the lot so far, right? Well, it got even better today. Some rich guy from D.C. saw my ad online and came all the way out from his beach house in St. Michaels and actually bought that old 'Vette I've had on the lot for months! Almost full asking price, too!"

"Really?" Brooke's mother sounded interested now. "That's wonderful, sweetie."

"You're telling me." He grinned. "And don't worry, I'm planning to spread the joy around. Ta-da!" He ducked into the hallway, returning a moment later holding a large shopping bag emblazoned with the cheerful logo of the area's largest toy store.

"Yay!" the twins cheered when they looked inside. "Thanks, Daddy!"

"And for my favorite wife, I made reservations next Saturday night at that Italian place you like in Ocean City. We'll make a weekend of it—I already called my sister, and she'll keep the twins while we're gone."

Brooke's mother gasped. "Oh, Roger!"

Brooke liked seeing her mother's face light up as she grabbed her husband and kissed him, gushing about the restaurant and the romantic time they'd have. She liked seeing the twins so happy, too. But her stomach tightened as she realized her stepfather hadn't mentioned what *she'd* be doing that weekend, and she couldn't help wondering if she'd been forgotten once again. . . .

"Don't worry, Brookie, I saved the best for last." Her stepfather turned to her with a wink. "See, that rich guy who bought the car told me he's whisking his whole family off on a surprise trip to Paris. That's why he was in such a hurry to make this deal—I guess they're leaving in a couple of days."

"Um, okay," Brooke said, a bit confused. Was her stepfather taking her to Paris? Somehow she doubted it.

"So the guy also told me his daughter had to pull out of her annual horse camp to go on the trip," her stepfather continued. "That means there's a spot open at her very exclusive camp, which happens to be located less than an hour from here." He grinned. "At least, there *was* a spot open, until I called and signed you and Foxy up for it!"

"What?" Brooke blurted out, still not quite understanding.

"Surprise!" her stepfather sang out. "You and Foxy are going away to Camp Pocomoke for two weeks. You leave on Sunday."

◆ CHAPTER ◆ 3

AN HOUR LATER, BROOKE STILL HADN'T quite wrapped her mind around her stepfather's big surprise. She picked at her dinner, occasionally sneaking a peek at him, studying his broad, ruddy face as if she'd never seen it before. And in a way, she felt as if she hadn't. He hardly seemed to notice her most of the time, and paid even less attention to Foxy unless he was complaining about how much she cost to keep.

And now this! Brooke was touched that her stepfather had thought of doing something like this for her. Sure, it had kind of fallen into his lap. But he could have ignored the open spot at horse camp and bought her a new cell phone or something else instead. After all, a two-week horse camp couldn't be cheap.

Two weeks. The thought of it struck her suddenly, causing her stomach to tighten so much, she put down her fork and swallowed hard to keep the bite of potato she'd just eaten from coming back up. Two whole weeks. Brooke had never spent more than a night or two away from her family before, and now she was supposed to spend two weeks all alone in a strange place.

But I won't be alone, she thought. *Foxy will be there with me.*

That made her feel better, but only a little. She needed to "speak" to her Pony Post friends—and now she had much bigger news to share than her silly self-training plans!

"May I be excused?" she asked, pushing her plate away.

Her stepfather looked up from shoveling chicken into his mouth. "Sure thing, honey," he said. "Better get upstairs and start packing, eh?"

"Yeah." Brooke smiled back. "Thanks again, Dad."

Upstairs, she pulled out her laptop and logged on to

the Pony Post. She was surprised to see that all three of her friends' names had little green dots glowing next to them. That meant they were all logged in to the site right now! That didn't happen very often unless they all set up a time beforehand, since they were in three different time zones.

Brooke quickly started typing, not wanting any of her friends to log off before she got her news out.

[BROOKE] Hi all! Guess what?

[MADDIE] BROOKE! Was wondering where u were all day. What's up?

[HALEY] Hi Brooke! How's Foxy?

[NINA] Hey B! Is it hot where you are? B/c it's hotter than Hades here in NOLA.

[HALEY] Isn't it always hot there? lol

[BROOKE] Hot here too. But listen, I have big news.

[HALEY] What?

[MADDIE] Spill!

[NINA] Is it about Foxy?

[BROOKE] Yes, sort of. My stepdad just gave me a big surprise—he's sending me & Foxy to riding camp!

[MADDIE] 2 COOL!

[NINA] Is it a sleepaway camp?

[BROOKE] Yes, for 2 wks.

[HALEY] That's amazing! I did riding camp last summer, but it was only day camp at my dressage trainer's barn.

[**NINA**] I've never done a riding camp, but I've been to sleepaway art camp and it was the BESTBESTBEST thing ever!

[**MADDIE**] I've been to soccer camp a few times. Rly fun! But riding camp? I'm super-jealous!!!!!

[**HALEY**] Me too! You're going to learn sooooo much!

Brooke smiled as she read over her friends' comments. They were making her feel less nervous already, mostly because she'd realized something. This was a *riding* camp, which meant all the other campers would be just as horse crazy as she was. Maybe she'd meet some girls like her Pony Post friends!

Well, not *exactly* like them, of course. They were all one of a kind. But if Brooke imagined spending two weeks with girls *almost* like Nina, Maddie, and Haley, the whole idea of camp suddenly seemed a lot less scary—and a lot more fun.

[BROOKE] Yah, I can't wait. This should be the perfect chance for me & Foxy to get more real training.

[HALEY] Xlnt! What will u be working on?

[MADDIE] More jumping maybe?

[BROOKE] I'm not sure—I don't rly know anything about the camp yet. But remember Foxy is still pretty green, so I'm sure whatever we work on will be good for her. And me, too!

They all chatted for a few more minutes, and then Nina had to log off to set the table for dinner, and Haley needed to go feed her pony. Brooke and Maddie said good-bye, too.

After she logged off the Pony Post site, Brooke pulled up a search engine and typed in the name of the camp. Camp Pocomoke had a website, but Brooke was disappointed to find that it wasn't very detailed. There were only a few photos, including one of a teenage girl jumping a big bay horse in a tidy riding ring and a couple of distant shots of barns and paddocks. Still, at least the site included an address, and when Brooke located the camp on a mapping site, she recognized the general area right away. It was a beautiful, unspoiled part of the peninsula near Pocomoke Sound. Brooke's family had visited several of the parks and small towns nearby, and there was lots of wildlife around and some great spots for hiking and camping.

Brooke put down the computer and headed out to the barn. The sun was sinking toward the western horizon, but it was still hot. Foxy was dozing under the oak tree across the fence from the draft horses. But the pony pricked her ears and wandered over when Brooke ducked under the fence.

"Guess what, baby girl?" Brooke whispered, sliding her arms around the mare's neck and breathing in her familiar scent. "We're going to camp! And we're going to learn a lot, and make new friends, and have lots of fun. . . ."

"Are you sure you don't want any dessert, sweetie?" Brooke's mother asked as she set bowls of ice cream in front of the twins.

Brooke shook her head. It was the big day, and she'd had a whole herd of butterflies in her stomach since the moment she'd woken up that morning. It had been all she could do to choke down a few bites of her tuna sandwich at lunch, and she'd done little more than push the food around on her plate during the family's early dinner.

Her stepfather hurried into the kitchen. "Trailer's hitched up," he announced, wiping his hands on a dish towel hanging on the back of a chair. "Ready to roll?"

"Almost." Brooke glanced at her watch, which she'd actually remembered to put on for once. Adam should have showed up by now, but there was no sign of him. "Um, but I should probably put my stuff in the car first."

"You haven't done that yet?" Brooke's mother sounded alarmed. "Go, do it! We need to be back here at a reasonable hour—I'm supposed to lead the church group meeting tonight, remember?"

Brooke wasn't sure how she was supposed to forget. Her mother had only mentioned it about fifty times. "Okay, okay. I put my saddle and barn stuff in earlier, so the rest will only take me a minute."

She hurried out into the living room, where she'd piled her suitcase, duffel, and sleeping bag beside the door. She grabbed her pillow off the top of the pile and stepped outside, squinting in the late-afternoon sunlight. A small stock trailer was parked in the driveway, hitched to one of the big diesel pickups from the used car lot. The trailer wasn't fancy, but Brooke knew she was lucky they had one at all. The only reason her parents had bought it was that it doubled as a way for her stepfather to haul car parts around. And it worked well enough for that as well as for Foxy.

I just hope Foxy remembers how to load, Brooke thought, hugging her pillow to her chest. The mare hadn't been near the trailer in over a year. Brooke had wanted to practice a couple of times before leaving for Camp Pocomoke, but her stepfather had been storing a spare engine or something in the trailer, and by the time he got around to unloading it, they'd run out of time.

After she'd finished loading her stuff, Brooke glanced up the road, hoping Adam hadn't forgotten today was the day. She'd texted him that morning to remind him, and he'd promised to come by to help on his way home from the pool. Even though he wasn't that interested in horses, he was the one who'd helped Brooke train Foxy to load in the first place when Foxy was two. Brooke's first few tentative attempts to teach the pony to get into the trailer hadn't gone that well—Brooke had been nervous and uncertain, and Foxy had picked up on that and refused to go anywhere near the scary metal monster parked in her pasture.

When Brooke had complained to Adam about it, he'd seen it as an interesting challenge. After watching a few videos and reading some online articles, he'd convinced the pony to get into the trailer on his very first try. Brooke had been amazed, and envious. It didn't seem fair that he could teach Foxy something she couldn't.

Still, the important thing was that he'd done it. And for a year or so after that, Brooke had practiced leading Foxy into and out of the trailer as often as she could, even if they weren't going anywhere. Sometimes she'd even feed the pony her dinner in there just to make it seem like a good place to be.

But then things had gotten busier at the car lot and Brooke's stepfather had needed the trailer more often, and it had just seemed easier to keep it there instead of at home. That had been the end of Foxy's trailer-loading practice.

Her stepfather burst out onto the front step, startling Brooke out of her thoughts. "Ready? Grab the pony and let's load up."

Brooke glanced up and down the street again. "Adam's supposed to come help me get her on the trailer," she said. "I'm sure he'll be here soon."

Her mother emerged in time to hear her. "We can't wait much longer. Here, text him and see if he's on his way."

She handed Brooke her smartphone. Brooke quickly sent Adam a text:

`Where r u? It's time to load Foxy.`

She stood there, holding her mother's phone. Her stepfather climbed into the truck and started the engine. He left it idling and hopped out again.

"Well?" he called.

At that moment the phone buzzed in Brooke's hand. It was a return text from Adam:

`Sry, forgot. Went to town w/ the guys after practice.`

Brooke gritted her teeth as disappointment flooded through her. What had happened to Adam? A year ago, he never would have let her down like this!

But she pushed those thoughts aside. What was the point in dwelling on them? "He's not coming," she told her parents. "I guess I'll have to load her by myself."

That turned out to be easier said than done. Foxy followed her willingly out to the front yard. But as soon as Brooke turned her toward the open trailer door, the mare planted her feet and snorted as if the trailer was a horse-eating dragon.

"What's wrong with Foxy?" Emma called out from the front step, where both twins were sitting, watching the show.

Brooke didn't answer. "Come on, girl," she said into Foxy's ear. "You can do this."

She turned the mare in a circle and tried again. And again. Each time, the mare stopped and refused to go any farther, no matter how hard Brooke pulled on her halter.

"What's the problem, Brooke?" Her stepfather sounded impatient. "We can't do this all afternoon."

"I know, sorry." Brooke took a deep breath, trying not to cry. Why did Foxy have to be so stubborn right now? "I just can't get her to go on."

"Here, let me try." Her stepfather strode over and grabbed the lead rope out of her hand. Before Brooke could protest—he didn't know what he was doing, he was going to scare Foxy—he'd given a cluck and a firm tug on the rope.

Foxy tossed her head and backed up a step. Brooke's stepfather reached back and smacked the mare on the rump with his free hand. That startled the mare forward, and before she—or Brooke—quite realized what was happening, Foxy was in the trailer.

"See?" Brooke's stepfather sounded satisfied as he quickly tied the mare and hopped out to swing the door shut. "It doesn't have to be such a drama."

"Yeah. Thanks." Brooke peered into the trailer through the slats. Now that Foxy was aboard, she didn't seem nervous at all. She was already nosing at the hay Brooke had stuffed into the hayrack earlier.

Brooke sighed. It was a good thing she and Foxy were going to camp, because they both obviously needed some work.

CHAPTER

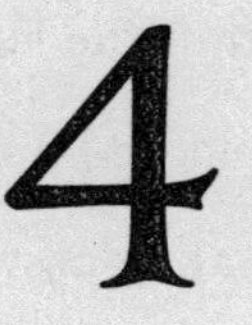

"OH, THIS AREA IS SO LOVELY." BROOKE'S mother peered out the front windshield. "Isn't it nice, Brooke? You're just a few miles from Pocomoke Sound here. Look, there's the sign. Turn here, Roger."

Brooke glanced back to check on Foxy, though she couldn't see much from the truck—just the tips of the mare's ears between the slats of the trailer. Then she leaned forward to check out the sign. It was fancier-looking than she'd expected, with the words POCOMOKE STABLES spelled out in fancy gold letters. Below that, smaller letters read BOARDING TRAINING SALES. The driveway was lined with twin rows of tall shade trees, beyond which Brooke caught a glimpse of sleek horses grazing in large, grassy pastures.

"Nice place," her stepfather said approvingly as they rounded a curve in the driveway and the rest of the farm came into view.

Brooke nodded. Off to the left was a huge riding ring with neatly raked footing and a course of colorful jumps. A woman was riding a tall, glossy chestnut horse in circles at the far end. Just past the ring was the barn, which was long and low and at least twice the size of the one where Brooke had taken riding lessons. One end opened onto a large paved courtyard, and on the far side of that stood the main house, a two-story brick Colonial with tidy black shutters and a deep front porch. There were several smaller outbuildings scattered around, but Brooke didn't take in the details.

"Yes, very nice," her mother was saying. "I didn't realize it was such a fancy place."

"Only the best for our girl, eh?" Brooke's stepfather tossed Brooke a wink in the rearview, then returned his focus to driving. "Suppose I should pull up over there, near the barn?"

"Um, I guess so." Brooke was watching as the woman in the ring turned her horse and sent him over one of the jumps, which the horse cleared easily. Nearby, Brooke noticed a second woman watching from the rail. She was on foot but dressed in riding clothes that matched those of her friend—beige breeches, tall boots, and a polo shirt.

Brooke swallowed hard, feeling intimidated. What kind of place was this? It certainly didn't look anything like the summer camps she'd seen in the movies. It wasn't anything much like the camps her Pony Post friends had described either. So far, she didn't even see any other kids!

As her father pulled into the courtyard, a woman hurried out of the barn, waving and smiling. She looked to be in her early fifties, with chin-length brown hair, and she was dressed in jeans and paddock boots. "Hi, I'm Robin Montgomery," she called. "You must be the Rhodeses."

Brooke's stepfather leaned out the truck's open window. "That's us," he replied cheerfully. "Where do you want the pony?"

The next few minutes were so busy that Brooke barely had time to breathe, let alone worry about what she was in for. Robin directed them to park at the end of the barn near a pair of sliding doors, then helped unload Foxy, who was wide-eyed and alert as she took in her new surroundings. After a moment the pony whinnied loudly, then spun around at the end of the lead rope.

"Sorry," Brooke said breathlessly, doing her best to hang on to the prancing pony. "She's not usually like this. She doesn't go new places very often."

"It's all right. Here, let me help." Robin took the lead from Brooke's hand, talking soothingly to Foxy. The mare remained alert, but stopped jumping around. Brooke stepped back, pushing her glasses up her nose. Even though Robin was being nice about it, Brooke couldn't help being embarrassed that Foxy was acting so nutty.

"Good, looks like everything's under control," Brooke's stepfather said. "Let's get your bags and stuff out, and then we've got to get back on the road." He turned and smiled apologetically at Robin. "My wife has an appointment this evening, so I'm afraid we can't hang around for the grand tour."

"Yes, that's right." Brooke's mother peered in through

the truck window at the twins, who had been sound asleep in the backseat for the past hour. "Besides, we don't want to wake up our younger kids."

"No worries," Robin replied. "Go ahead and grab your things, Brooke. The other girls are in the barn—they can show you to the bunkhouse once we get Foxy settled in."

The other girls. Brooke swallowed hard, not sure whether to be excited or nervous. Somehow she couldn't imagine girls like her Pony Post friends hanging around a fancy stable like this! "Um, okay," she said.

Before she knew it, the truck and trailer were disappearing down the long drive and Brooke was on her own. Well, except for Foxy, who still wasn't acting at all like her usual placid, unflappable self.

"She really isn't spooky, normally," Brooke told Robin as the pony jumped and stared bug-eyed at a leaf blowing across the courtyard.

Robin smiled, which made the corners of her bright blue eyes crinkle in a nice way. "I understand. This is all new for her. I'm sure she'll adjust."

She sounded very sympathetic, which made Brooke

feel a little better. Just then a girl appeared at the open end of the barn.

"Oh, is the new camper here?" she asked Robin, staring curiously at Brooke. "Hi, I'm Livi."

"Hi. Brooke." Brooke felt self-conscious. Livi looked just as fancy as the rest of this place. She was Brooke's age or maybe a little older, tall and pretty, with sleek blond hair and wide hazel eyes. Her spotless breeches and sleeveless lavender polo made Brooke feel as if she should tuck her T-shirt into her shorts and rub the dried mud off her sneakers, though she resisted the urge.

"Cool. Nice to meet you, Brooke. Is that your horse?" Livi sounded surprised as she turned her gaze to Foxy. "She's cute. Is she a pony?"

"Yes. A Chincoteague pony, actually."

"Oh, like in that movie or whatever, right? Shouldn't she have spots, though?"

Foxy whinnied loudly again, saving Brooke from having to answer. "We'd better get this girl settled in," Robin said. "It looks like Foxy's worked up a bit of a sweat. How about if I walk her a bit, let her check things out and eat a few bites of grass and settle down? In the meantime, Livi can introduce you to the others and they can help you move your things in." She nodded toward Brooke's pile of belongings, including her English saddle, which was perched precariously atop her suitcase, where her stepfather had set it.

"Are you sure?" Brooke blurted out, feeling a flash of panic at being separated from Foxy. Even though the pony was acting kind of nutty, Foxy felt like Brooke's only lifeline to normal right now. "I mean, I could walk her if you don't have time."

Robin smiled. "No, go on. It's fine. I'd like to get to know her, anyway. We'll meet you inside in a few minutes." With a cluck to Foxy, she started off across the courtyard, heading for the grassy, tree-dotted lawn beyond.

"Come on, the others are inside," Livi said. Tossing her blond hair over her shoulder, she spun on one polished paddock boot and headed back into the barn.

Brooke followed. Compared to the bright, hot summer day outside, the barn felt shady and pleasant. A stout dapple-gray horse was cross-tied in the aisle while an older and equally stout woman fussed over him with a currycomb.

"'Scuse us," Livi sang out, ducking under the tie on one side.

"What was all the commotion out there?" the woman asked.

"You mean the whinnying? That's Brooke's pony." Livi waved a hand at Brooke. "They're both new campers this year."

"Ah!" The woman smiled at Brooke. "Welcome to Pocomoke Stables—I mean Camp Pocomoke." She tittered. "It's always such fun for us boring old boarders to see the things you girls get up to!"

"Thanks." Brooke smiled uncertainly, then followed Livi, who was already hurrying ahead, calling to two other girls halfway down the aisle. When Brooke reached them, they immediately gathered around, making Brooke feel surrounded even though there were only three of them.

"So Brooke, this is Paige and that's Hannah." Livi pointed to each of the other girls in turn. Paige was petite and pale, with bright red hair that hung in waves around her shoulders. Hannah was African-American and even taller than Livi, with wide-set eyes and sleek dark hair pulled into a short ponytail.

"Hi," Paige said, tucking a strand of red hair behind her ear. Her smile was big and friendly, and Brooke couldn't help smiling back. "Brooke, right? We were wondering when you'd get here."

"At least for the past hour, anyway. We actually didn't know you were coming until we got here ourselves," Livi put in with a giggle.

"Yeah." Hannah was studying Brooke with a slightly puzzled look on her face. "I mean, of course Lauren texted us when she found out she had to cancel. But we didn't think Robin would find anyone to take her place at the last minute."

"But we're glad you're here," Paige added quickly. "You're going to have a blast. This place is the best!"

Livi nodded vigorously. "Totally! Royal and I—that's my horse, Royal—we went from doing the pre–children's hunters to the children's after camp last summer, all because of Robin. She's an awesome trainer. Did you know she was long-listed for the Olympic team once?"

"Of course she knows that." Hannah rolled her eyes.

"Everyone knows that. That's probably why she wanted to come, right, Brooke?"

Brooke wasn't sure what to say. She didn't want these girls to know how out of place she felt. Then again, they'd figure it out sooner or later. Probably sooner.

"Not exactly," she admitted, staring at Hannah's crystal-studded belt to avoid meeting any of their eyes. "Um, I'm not really into showing and stuff."

"Oh!" Livi's eyes widened in surprise. "But then why—"

Paige elbowed her. "Never mind," she said. "You'll have fun anyway. Robin teaches all kinds of people and horses. She's amazing."

The other two nodded. Brooke smiled weakly. "Okay. Thanks."

To her relief, the others seemed to lose interest in her after that, turning their chatter to other topics, full of names she didn't recognize and stuff she didn't care about. Brooke stopped listening after a while, focusing instead on looking around the barn. The older woman finished her grooming session and led her gelding into a stall, then disappeared. A cat crept out of one empty stall and into another, tail twitching. Several horses, all of them tall and sleek and gorgeous, hung their heads out over the stall doors.

Finally a teenage girl who looked a couple of years older than the others wandered in. "Hey, whose stuff is that in the courtyard?" she called out. "We're going to try to get a ride in before dark—Robin said it's okay—and if you don't want your suitcase stepped on . . ."

"Oops!" Livi said. "Oh, right. Robin said we're supposed to help Brooke move in."

"Chill out, Jess!" Hannah called to the older girl. "We're moving it."

"Whatever." The older girl let herself into a stall nearby.

"That's one of the olders," Livi told Brooke.

At Brooke's confused look, Paige giggled. "Older campers, she means," she said. "We're the youngers, they're the olders—fourteen and up."

"Yeah. Except Robin has to change the age rule next year so I can stay with you guys," Hannah said. "No way do I want to be stuck with those losers!"

They all laughed. Brooke smiled weakly. "Um, my stuff . . ."

"Yeah, we're on it. Come on." Paige dashed off down the aisle with the other two on her heels.

By the time Brooke caught up, Hannah had already picked up Brooke's saddle. "What brand is this?" she asked. "Is it a close contact?"

"Um, I don't know. The lady at the store said it was made in England, I think?" Brooke wasn't about to explain how she'd saved up for almost a year to buy the saddle at the local consignment shop, or how it had been the only one in her price range that wasn't actually coming apart at the seams.

"Made in England is good," Paige said quickly. "I mean, mine was made in France, but I also looked at some from England. Come on, the bunkhouse is this way." She grabbed Brooke's duffel and slung it over her shoulder, pulling her red hair out from under the strap in one smooth, practiced movement.

Livi was already wandering off with Brooke's suitcase and grooming bucket. Brooke picked up her sleeping bag and pillow and followed.

The other girls led her to a cute clapboard cabin behind the barn. It had green trim and a lush rose vine clambering up one side and over the roof, the soft flowery scent of the pink blossoms filling the air.

"Isn't this cool?" Livi said over her shoulder. "The olders are stuck in Bunkhouse A, which is bigger and has a bathtub, but it's way over on the other side of the house."

"Yeah, I'd much rather be near the horses," Paige added, waving a hand at the barn just a few yards away, across a narrow strip of lawn.

Hannah shrugged, patting her dark hair. "I don't know—I wouldn't mind having a bathtub."

"You'd *need* the tub if you were in Bunk A," Livi said with a giggle. "Because if you were that close to the house, your horrible off-key singing in the shower would totally wake Robin up!"

That made all three of them laugh. Brooke forced a smile. It was pretty obvious that these girls were good friends. Where did that leave her?

The cabin was basically one large room with four bunks. Suitcases, clothes, and other things were strewn across all four of the beds.

"Oops, guess we'd better move our stuff off Brooke's

bed." Paige quickly grabbed a couple of shirts and tossed them onto one of the other bunks.

Hannah picked up a pair of breeches. "Yeah, sorry," she told Brooke. "Like we said, we didn't know you were coming at first."

Livi giggled. "We were figuring we'd use Lauren's bunk as our closet this year."

"But there—now it's all yours." Paige grabbed one last handful of clothes, then kicked a pair of tall riding boots out of the way.

"Hey, those are my new customs!" Livi protested, swooping in to rescue the boots.

Meanwhile Hannah dumped Brooke's saddle on the bed. "You should probably unpack later," she said. "Come show us your horse!"

"It's a pony," Livi informed the other two. "A Chincoteague pony. Like the movie."

"You mean the book?" Paige said. "*Misty of Chincoteague*. I read that when I was younger—it takes place near here. And it's totally based on a true story. Morgan told us she went to watch them swim across the water once, remember?"

Brooke had no idea who Morgan was. Probably another good friend she didn't know. "Right," she said. "That's where I got Foxy. We went to the pony penning and bought her at the auction."

"Really? I never heard of anyone doing that." Paige smiled. "Well, except in the book, I mean."

"Chincoteagues are kind of a rare breed, right?" Hannah put in. "Was your pony really expensive?"

Brooke hesitated, not sure how to answer that. Foxy had seemed expensive to her, but she had a feeling these girls might have a different definition of the term.

"Um, not really," she said.

Luckily, the others didn't seem interested in the details. They headed out of the bunkhouse and back over to the barn, arriving just in time to meet Robin as she led Foxy inside. Brooke was relieved to see that her pony seemed calmer. Foxy was walking obediently at Robin's side, looking with interest at the stalled horses on either side of the aisle.

"Perfect timing," Robin said when she saw Brooke. "Foxy is feeling better about things now, I think. You can take her to her stall and let her relax for a while." She glanced at Paige. "Show her the empty stall next to Snow."

Foxy was going to stay in a stall? Somehow Brooke hadn't been expecting that. She took the lead from Robin, who hurried off down the aisle.

"Cool, Snow is my horse—we'll be neighbors!" Paige said brightly. "Come on, it's this way."

Brooke bit her lip and glanced at her pony. Foxy had never been shut in a stall in her life. The only time the mare had ever spent the night indoors was the previous fall, when a hurricane had passed over the peninsula and she'd gone to stay with the neighbors' draft horses in their big, open barn. How would she handle being stuck in a small stall, all by herself?

Maybe it will be fine, Brooke told herself. *She didn't mind being in the trailer, and that's even smaller, right?*

Paige led the way to an empty stall. Next door was a tall, elegant gray mare with a short mane. "That's Snow," Livi informed Brooke.

"She's pretty." But Brooke wasn't focused on Paige's horse. She held her breath as she led Foxy into the empty stall beside Snow's and let her loose. Foxy stood there for a moment, and

Brooke quickly let herself out and shut the door.

"Want us to give you a tour of the rest of the farm?" Paige suggested. "We could show you where—"

She was interrupted by a loud whinny as Foxy leaped forward, stopping just short of the stall door. The pony shoved her head out into the aisle, her eyes rolling and her nostrils flared. Brooke reached out to pat her, but the mare whirled away.

"What's wrong with her?" Hannah wondered as Foxy spun in a circle before returning to the door.

Paige shrugged. "She's new here, that's all."

"Maybe," Brooke said. "Um, or maybe it's because she's not used to being in a stall."

Livi turned to stare at her. "What do you mean?"

Brooke chewed her lower lip as she watched her frantic pony. "She lives in a field with a run-in shed. I never shut her in. I never had a reason to before."

"Really?" Hannah sounded surprised. "Huh. Vegas would die if I forced him to live outside. He loves his cozy stall."

Foxy whinnied again and kicked the wall. Several of the other horses nickered or snorted in response. A moment later Robin returned, looking concerned.

"Everything all right?" she asked.

"I'm sorry. She's not used to being inside." Tears welled up in Brooke's eyes. "I didn't know she was going to have to stay in a stall, she's never done that before, and—"

Robin interrupted. "I see. Never mind, I have an idea."

She stepped forward, grabbing Foxy's halter the next time the mare leaped forward. Foxy shook her head and tried to back up, but gave up quickly when Robin hung on. The stable owner snapped a lead rope onto Foxy's halter and led her out of the stall.

"Where are you taking her?" Hannah asked.

"She can stay in Hero's stall." Robin glanced at Brooke. "Hero is one of my horses. His stall has a large attached run so he can move around more—he's older and has arthritis. Do you think Foxy will like that better?"

"I'm sure she will," Brooke said. "But is that okay? If your horse has arthritis, doesn't he need that stall?"

"It's fine," Robin assured her with a smile. "Hero is mostly retired—he can live outside for a couple of weeks."

"Really?" Livi said. "Won't he freak out?"

"Absolutely not," Robin replied. "He's lived out before.

Most horses actually like being outside, you know."

Paige giggled. "Not Vegas. Hannah's trainer says he's a hothouse flower."

"Hmm." Robin didn't really respond to that. She led Foxy down the aisle to a different stall. It was larger than the other one, and had a wide doorway at the back leading out to a narrow paddock overlooking the riding ring.

As soon as Robin released Foxy into the stall, the pony headed toward the paddock with her ears pricked. She trotted out through the door, head raised and ears swiveling in all directions.

"One of my boarders has the other run-out stall." Robin waved a hand at a large bay horse that was standing in an open doorway, looking out into an adjoining paddock. "So Foxy will have company whether she stays in or out."

"Thanks," Brooke said, relieved that her pony seemed much less upset already. "Sorry for all the trouble."

"No trouble at all." Robin's smile was wide and genuine. "Now let's go into the house for a snack and leave her to get settled. We can come back and check on her later."

◆ ◆ ◆

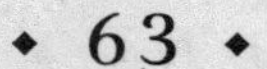

Later that evening, Brooke lay on her bunk and stared at the wooden ceiling beams. The other three girls had been chattering nonstop since returning to the cabin. They didn't even stop talking when one of them went into the tiny shared bathroom to shower and change into pajamas; they just talked louder so nobody would miss anything.

Once in a while one of them—usually Paige—made an effort to include Brooke, but mostly they seemed to forget she was there. From listening to the three-way conversation, Brooke had figured out that the other girls had been coming to this camp for the past three years, and that Camp Pocomoke was where the three of them had met. Hannah was from a fancy suburb of Baltimore; Paige lived in Virginia, south of Washington, D.C.; and Livi had come all the way from Pennsylvania, where her mother was a U.S. congresswoman. The three of them only saw one another at summer camp and the occasional horse show, which meant they had a lot of catching up to do.

Brooke yawned, wondering if the other girls were going to talk all night. Sleeping through their conversation couldn't be much harder than sleeping through one of

Ethan's tantrums or Emma's screaming fits, right?

The windows were open to let in the evening breeze, and Brooke smiled as she heard the faint sound of a horse nickering somewhere in the night. A second later another horse responded.

"I think that was Foxy," she said.

The other three girls turned to look at her. "What?" Livi said.

"That nicker." Brooke was starting to wish she'd kept the thought to herself. "I think it was Foxy. She has this really deep nicker, even though she's so small."

"Oh. That's cute," Paige said with a smile. "Snow pretty much sounds like every other horse when she nickers."

"Hmm." Brooke smiled back, but she was glad when the other three returned to their conversation. She could tell they were trying to be nice to her, but it was pretty obvious she didn't fit in, and neither did Foxy. Had coming here been a mistake?

◆ CHAPTER ◆
5

"RISE AND SHINE!" ROBIN POKED HER HEAD into the bunkhouse. "Breakfast starts in twenty minutes."

Brooke was already dressed. She'd slept fitfully and woken early. After creeping into the tiny bathroom to pull on jeans and a T-shirt, she'd been tempted to sneak over to the barn to check on Foxy. But she wasn't sure what the rules were here, and she was tired of sounding clueless to the others. Besides, Livi and Paige were still asleep, Livi snoring softly from beneath her pillow. Hannah was awake but still in bed. She'd mumbled a greeting to Brooke, then immediately pulled out her cell phone and started scrolling through her messages. Her dark hair was loose and sticking out around her head in soft curls that Brooke thought looked nicer than Hannah's usual sleek but severe ponytail, though she never would have dared to say so.

At Robin's voice, Livi's eyes opened and she rolled over. "Wha time is it?" she mumbled, spitting a stray strand of blond hair out of her mouth.

"Time to get up," Hannah replied. "Dibs on first shower."

"No!" Paige sat up too, suddenly wide-awake. She shoved a strand of tangled red hair out of her face. "Don't let Hans in the shower first, or she'll use all the hot water!"

Livi gasped. "Oh no, you're right!"

She leaped out of bed, tripping over her own slippers. Hannah was laughing as she grabbed a towel from the cubby at the foot of her bed and dashed toward the bathroom. Livi and Paige lunged after her. There was a brief tussle, which Livi won, slamming the door shut behind her as she disappeared inside.

"Cheater!" Hannah complained. "I called dibs."

Paige laughed and collapsed on the foot of Brooke's bed, which was nearest the bathroom door. "You had the right idea," she commented. "There's always a fight for the bathroom in the mornings. I just can't stand getting up any earlier than I have to."

"I usually like sleeping in too," Brooke said. "I guess I had a little trouble sleeping in a strange place."

Paige smiled sympathetically. "I was the same way when I first came here. Don't worry, before long Camp Pocomoke will feel like your home away from home."

Brooke returned the smile, but it felt a bit forced. So far, she couldn't imagine ever feeling at home in this place. But who knew? Maybe Paige was right. Maybe Brooke and Foxy would settle in sooner or later. Brooke hoped so, anyway.

Fifteen minutes later, all the girls were dressed. Brooke followed the others out of the cabin, expecting them to turn left toward the house. Instead, they headed across the narrow patch of grass between the bunkhouse and the barn.

"Aren't we going to breakfast?" Brooke asked.

"Yeah." Livi ran her fingers through her damp blond hair. "The *horses'* breakfast."

"Oh, right, we didn't tell you about that part, did we?" Paige said. "See, at Camp Pocomoke we're supposed to take care of our horses ourselves."

She, Livi, and Hannah gazed at Brooke as if expecting her to react somehow. "Okay," Brooke said cautiously.

Hannah rolled her eyes. "I know, right?" she said. "I mean, this place is great and all. But I could do without picking up horse poop before breakfast."

Paige giggled. "Don't let Robin hear you say that or she'll make you clean the whole barn instead of just Vegas's stall."

"Do you know what Foxy eats?" Livi asked Brooke. "If not, we can check with Robin—I'm sure your barn gave her all the details."

"My barn?" Brooke was confused. "Um, Foxy lives at my house. I feed her breakfast every day."

"Oh!" Paige nodded. "That's right, you said something about that yesterday. Well, then never mind—you'll be an old pro!"

Brooke could tell she was trying to be nice. So how come her comment—and the way Livi and Hannah were staring as if Brooke had three heads—made her feel like such a freak?

She forgot about that as they stepped into the barn.

It was bustling with activity. Several of the older campers were wandering around, carrying buckets or pitchforks. Robin was leading a horse out of its stall, and a younger woman with a wavy dark ponytail was pushing a wheelbarrow down the aisle.

"You're late," Robin announced when she saw Brooke's group enter.

"Sorry. Hannah took forever in the shower," Livi said.

Brooke didn't hear Robin's response, because at that moment Foxy stuck her head into the aisle and nickered. The mare's eyes were bright and her ears pricked forward—as if this was just like every other morning.

Brooke smiled, suddenly feeling a little less out of sorts. "Hey, girl," she said, stepping over to rub the pony's nose.

The young woman with the wheelbarrow stopped nearby and leaned on her pitchfork. "Is that your pony?" she asked. "Is she a Chincoteague?"

"Yes," Brooke said cautiously.

The young woman smiled. "Thought she might be. Had one myself when I was your age—picked him out at the pony penning when I was seven years old."

"Really? That's what I did too." Brooke smiled back. "Except I was eight."

Just then Robin walked by, leading a horse. "I see you've met Felicia," she told Brooke. "She's our part-time barn worker and she knows how everything works around here. So if you have a question and can't find me, she's a good person to ask."

"Oh, okay. Thanks." Brooke shot Felicia a shy smile. Was it weird that she already felt as if she had more in common with the barn worker than with the other campers? Pushing that thought aside, she hurried to the feed room to get Foxy's grain.

After the horses were fed and the stalls cleaned, the girls headed inside for their own breakfast. Robin's house managed to seem spacious and cozy at the same time, with comfortably elegant furnishings and lots of nooks and crannies filled with interesting things—antiques, books, knickknacks, framed photographs of horses and people. The sunny dining room had a hunt theme, with paintings and figurines of foxes and hounds everywhere Brooke looked. Several large windows overlooked one of the pastures.

"Over here," Paige said, pulling Brooke toward one end of the long mahogany table. The older campers were already sitting at the other end.

"Good morning, everyone," Robin said, taking a seat in the middle. She set a sheaf of papers in front of her. "Welcome to another year at Camp Pocomoke."

A cheer went up from both ends of the table. Paige added a loud whoop that made the others giggle.

"Now, I know most of you know the deal," Robin went on. "But we have a couple of new campers this year."

"Kayley isn't really new," protested one of the older campers, shoving a rosy-cheeked blond girl with her shoulder. "She just skipped last year, that's all."

"Nevertheless," Robin said. "I want to go over the basics. Even some of our more experienced campers might have forgotten a few things over the winter."

"She's talking about you, Livi," Hannah said in a loud stage whisper. Everyone laughed, including Livi. Brooke smiled along, even though she wasn't sure why that was funny.

"All right." Robin smiled. "Now, as usual, you're

divided into older and younger groups. You'll be together at mealtimes and for some non-riding activities, but separate for your riding and horsemanship lessons."

The other girls were all nodding along, looking slightly bored. Robin continued.

"As most of you know, my daughter Morgan won't be a counselor this year," she said. "She moved to New York City right after her college graduation last month, and she can't take time away from her new job."

There was a general murmur of disappointment. Robin paused and looked down for a moment, shuffling through the papers in front of her. Was that a look of sadness on her face? Brooke felt a flash of curiosity, but shrugged it off. Of course it made sense that Robin was sad—her daughter had recently moved away from home.

"Now, I've hired a local girl to help out in Morgan's place," Robin went on. "Her name is Abby, and I think you'll all like her. Preston will be coming in a couple of days to help out as well."

Paige leaned toward Brooke. "That's Robin's boyfriend," she whispered. "He's, like, some kind of superstar real estate guy or something. His cousin boards here—that's how he and Robin first met."

"This year's activities should be fun," Robin said. "As usual, one of the neighboring estates has graciously agreed to let us use their tennis courts and pool, and we'll also be setting up a visit to the local golf course for anyone who's interested. Abby mentioned volleyball and kickball as well, but I'll let her tell you about that when she arrives in a few minutes."

Brooke couldn't help being alarmed. She'd thought this camp was all about riding. She wasn't very interested in most other sports—not like Maddie the soccer freak, or Nina, who'd taken dance since she was little, or even Haley, who went hiking and camping and fishing and cross-country skiing with her family all the time.

Thinking of her Pony Post friends made Brooke feel wistful. If they were here with her, she'd be much more excited to try all those new things. She was sure the four of them would have a blast—and so would their ponies.

Maybe they'd even be able to ride out and find a deserted stretch of beach where they could pretend to be riding wild ponies on Assateague. . . .

Realizing that Robin was still talking, Brooke tuned back in: ". . . and I hope you'll all have fun and improve your riding and general horsemanship. As always, we'll be able to see just how much you've learned at our annual end-of-camp horse show."

Once again, several of the other campers cheered. Robin smiled.

"Olders, Abby will take you for a quick swim as soon as she gets here, so go get changed. Youngers, you're with me—your first riding lesson starts in twenty minutes. I want to see what kind of progress you've all made since last summer." Glancing at Brooke, she added, "And of course, I'll want to evaluate our new pair."

Brooke felt a nervous shiver run through her. She and Foxy had never been "evaluated" before. She wasn't even quite sure what that meant.

"Now get to the barn and start grooming and tacking

up," Robin finished. "I'll expect you in the ring in"—she paused and checked her watch—"nineteen and a half minutes."

"More inside leg, Brooke!" Robin called as Brooke and Foxy rounded the short end of the ring. "You need to ask her to bend through the turn, but you can't do it all with your reins."

"Sorry." Brooke felt flustered as she tried to do what Robin was asking. "Um, we haven't really practiced that kind of thing much yet."

So far her first riding lesson at Camp Pocomoke wasn't going very well. It was pretty obvious that the other girls' horses were much better trained than Foxy, and the girls themselves much better trained than Brooke.

"Everyone, let's halt and talk about this," Robin called out.

The other three riders came to the middle. Brooke felt short beside their horses. All of them were at least a hand taller than Foxy. Hannah's horse, Vegas, a handsome chestnut warmblood, was a full seventeen hands!

"Now let's discuss bending and why we do it," Robin began. "When we ask a horse to use its body properly . . ."

She went on for a while, occasionally asking questions that the other girls answered easily. Brooke listened, trying to take it all in, but she couldn't help feeling self-conscious and distracted. It was obvious that she and Foxy didn't belong here any more than Ethan and Emma belonged in a college philosophy class, and everyone knew it. Brooke guessed that Robin hadn't planned to cover such basic material during this lesson. The other girls didn't say anything about it, but Brooke was pretty sure she caught them exchanging meaningful glances a few times.

By the end of the lesson, all she wanted was to get away and figure out how she was going to survive two weeks of this. She untacked Foxy quickly and snapped a lead rope on her halter.

"Is it okay if I take Foxy out to graze for a few minutes?" she asked Robin.

"Sure, go ahead," Robin said.

Paige looked up from picking her horse's hoof. "I'll come too," she said. "Snow loves hand grazing."

Brooke's heart sank. So much for being alone! She forced a smile. "Okay."

Soon both girls were watching their horses nibble grass behind the barn. Paige leaned against her mare's shoulder and gave Brooke a sidelong look.

"Robin can be tough, but she really knows her stuff," she said. "You'll be surprised how fast you and Foxy will learn."

"Okay." Brooke didn't meet her eye.

Paige was silent for a moment. Then she cleared her throat. "So I know you said you don't show, and I noticed you only brought that schooling helmet. If you want, you can borrow my spare helmet for the show at the end of camp."

Brooke's free hand flew to her head. She'd been in such a hurry to get away that she'd forgotten to take off her helmet, which had been a ninth-birthday gift from her mother. After three years of nearly daily wear, it looked slightly threadbare, though Brooke hadn't really realized it until that moment.

"What's wrong with my helmet?" she snapped.

Paige looked worried. "Um, nothing. It's just that most people don't wear that kind for showing these days, and I thought you'd want to fit in, so . . ."

Suddenly Brooke couldn't take any more. "I have to

go," she choked out, willing herself not to start crying in front of the other girl. She grabbed a chunk of Foxy's mane and vaulted onto her back.

The pony lifted her head from the grass, startled. "Hey," Paige said. "What are you doing?"

"Just going for a ride." Brooke gave Foxy a kick, and the pony jumped into a trot. Using her legs and a couple of tugs on the lead rope, Brooke sent her down a lane leading off between two large pastures. Paige called her name a couple of times, but Brooke didn't look back.

She felt better once the barn was out of sight behind her. Letting Foxy slow to a walk, Brooke glanced around. They were passing the far edge of Robin's largest pasture. Beyond that lay a tangle of scrubby brush with colorful birds flitting around. Off to the left was a farm field—soybeans, like the place across the road from Brooke's house. On the far side of the field was forest.

"This is more like it," Brooke murmured, causing Foxy to flick an ear back briefly. "We might not know how to bend properly in the ring or jump big fences or do fancy dressage moves. But who needs that stuff, anyway?"

The farther they got from Pocomoke Stables, the more relaxed she felt. After skirting the soybean field, Brooke found a winding trail leading into the woods. Not long after that, the trees thinned out and she heard the distant sound of crying gulls and breaking waves.

"Sounds like we found the Sound," she told Foxy. They kept going and soon crested a sandy hill overlooking a dirt road that ran parallel to the woods. On the other side of the road, a slope covered in wild grasses led down to the rocky shoreline. Brooke sat back and tightened her seat and Foxy halted. For a moment they both surveyed the beautiful, wild scene. A shorebird flew up in a flurry of wings while the gulls Brooke had heard earlier wheeled and shrieked far overhead. A sailboat skidded by in the distance, looking like something on a postcard.

Brooke squeezed lightly, and Foxy picked her way down the slope, pushing through the marshy grasses. Brooke sucked in a deep breath of briny air, imagining that this must be what it was like to ride along the wild shores of Assateague Island. . . .

"Hey!" A sharp voice broke into her reverie.

Brooke jumped, then realized Foxy already must have noticed that they weren't alone. The pony was staring, ears pricked, at a pair of people picking their way across the rocks nearby. In the lead was an elderly woman with a cane, dressed in a shabby cotton sweater and orthopedic shoes. Right behind her was a teenage girl dressed in normal shorts and a T-shirt.

"Miss Alice, slow down!" the girl called. "You'll kill yourself on those rocks!"

The old woman ignored her. "What are you doing here?" she demanded, waving her cane at Brooke. "This is private property. You're trespassing!"

"S-sorry." Brooke tightened her grip on Foxy's mane as the pony took a step backward, eyeing the woman and her cane warily.

"Sorry doesn't pay the mortgage!" the old woman snapped, her watery blue eyes flashing with fury.

By now the teenage girl had caught up. "Leave her alone, okay?" she said. Glancing up at Brooke, she rolled her eyes. "Sorry. She thinks everyone is a developer sneaking around, trying to steal her land." She poked the old woman on the shoulder. "She's just a girl on a pony, okay? No need to call the police."

"I'm really sorry," Brooke said again. "I didn't know we were trespassing."

"It's no biggie," the girl said. "Your pony's cute. Is she a Welsh cross or what?"

"No, she's a Chincoteague pony," Brooke said.

"Harrumph. Chincoteague, eh?" The old woman cast a curious glance at Foxy, then turned away. "Don't let me catch you here again, girl."

"You won't. I'm sorry." Brooke turned Foxy around and rode as quickly as she could back the way they'd come, not daring to look back.

As Brooke and Foxy approached the barn half an hour later, Livi rushed out and waved at them.

"She's back! Hey, Robin, Brooke's back!" the blond girl shouted.

She hurried forward. Paige and Hannah emerged

from the barn and rushed after her. Soon all three of them were dancing along beside Foxy, keyed up and extra-talkative.

"Wow, I've never seen Robin so freaked-out," Hannah commented. "She thinks you're, like, dead or something."

"We were worried too," Livi added.

"Yeah," Paige said. "Why'd you ride off like that?"

Before Brooke could answer, Robin rushed out, her expression pinched and anxious. "Brooke!" she exclaimed. "Thank goodness! What were you thinking, riding off alone like that?"

Brooke was taken aback. "I ride alone all the time at home," she said. As Robin's frown deepened, Brooke quickly added, "But I'm sorry. I didn't realize it was against the rules."

Robin glanced at the other girls. "All right, she's obviously alive. Now get back to your tack cleaning—it's almost time for lunch."

As the trio wandered off, whispering to one another, Brooke slid down from Foxy's back. "I'm really sorry," she told Robin. "I didn't mean to make you worry. We just rode down to the water."

"The water?" Robin said. "That's several miles away."

Brooke nodded, thinking back on the ride. "We ran into an old woman on the shore," she said. "She seemed kind of, um, cranky."

"An old woman? What did she look like?"

Brooke described the woman as best she could. "There was a girl with her too. Maybe fifteen or sixteen? She called the woman Miss Alice."

"Oh." Robin's expression cleared. "Yes, that would be Alice Foster. She lives in an old house overlooking the water—her family has owned the property for generations. But she lives alone, so I have no idea who the girl could have been."

Just then one of the adult boarders emerged from the barn. She flashed a quick, distracted smile in Brooke's direction, then started babbling at Robin about a stone in her horse's shoe.

"Be right there," Robin told the woman. "Brooke, put Foxy in the pasture and get washed up for lunch."

Brooke nodded, giving a tug on Foxy's lead as the barn owner hurried away. "Come on, girl," she said. "The fun's over."

Foxy nickered, and Brooke smiled and rubbed her nose. Despite how their adventure had turned out, she couldn't quite be sorry she'd had it.

◆ CHAPTER ◆ 6

MONDAY AFTERNOON PASSED QUICKLY FOR Brooke. After lunch, the younger campers went swimming and then had a horsemanship lesson. Unlike in the riding lesson, Brooke had no trouble keeping up, thanks to her lifelong habit of reading everything she could about horses. Robin complimented her several times on her knowledge, and the other girls seemed impressed too.

That evening, after feeding the horses and having their own dinner, the whole group gathered in the living room to watch some horse videos, and by the time they'd finished, everyone was yawning. Brooke fell asleep almost as soon as her head hit her pillow, feeling only the slightest pangs of homesickness and thinking that maybe camp wouldn't be so bad after all.

But the next morning after breakfast, she was dismayed to discover that the younger campers were scheduled to spend the morning playing tennis.

"It'll be awesome!" exclaimed Abby, the counselor. She was a college student with short straw-colored hair, a snub nose sprinkled with freckles, and an enthusiastic attitude about everything. "Come on, gang, let's hit the courts!"

The girls piled into Robin's old minivan and Abby drove them a few miles down the road to the same estate where they'd gone swimming the day before. Brooke glanced longingly at the pool as they passed it.

"I wish we were going swimming again instead," she murmured.

She was talking to herself more than to the others, but Paige heard her. "Don't you like tennis?" she asked.

Brooke shrugged. "I'm not sure. I've never really played before except a couple of times, goofing off at the park."

She thought back a few summers to the day she and Adam had taught themselves to play using his parents' old racquets. They'd spent more time trying to hit each other with the ball than actually following the rules. It had been fun—the kind of fun she and Adam used to have together all the time.

Brooke's smile faded as she tuned back in to the conversation in the van. The other girls were all discussing how long they'd been playing tennis, how many years of lessons they'd taken, and in Livi's case, how many junior tournaments she'd won playing doubles with her sister.

Yikes, Brooke thought. *I guess that's just one more thing they're all better at than me.*

"Maybe you guys should go ahead and play without me," she said. "I can just watch. I don't mind."

"No way, Brooke!" Abby sang out from the driver's seat. She pulled into a parking spot near the courts. "Life's for living, not for watching. It'll be fun!"

Brooke winced. She'd known Abby less than twenty-four hours, and she could already tell "It'll be fun!" was one of her favorite phrases.

"Yeah, you've got to play," Hannah added. "For one thing, we need four to play doubles."

Paige nodded. "You can be my partner, Brooke."

Brooke smiled weakly. "Um, okay."

It went about as well as Brooke might have predicted. The other girls all played as if they were warming up for Wimbledon, while Brooke didn't even know how to serve properly until Paige showed her. Even then, Brooke could barely get the ball across the net.

After her third or fourth flubbed serve, Brooke had had enough. As she hurried forward to retrieve the ball she'd just sent into the net, she feigned a stumble.

"Ow!" she said. "Um, I twisted my ankle. I'd better sit out for a while—I don't want to make it worse so I can't ride."

"Are you sure?" Abby looked as if she wanted to argue, but instead she bit her lip and glanced at the other three girls. Hannah and Livi were trading a look, and Paige was staring at the ground. Brooke had the feeling they all knew she was bluffing, but she didn't care. She gazed defiantly at Abby.

"I'm positive," she said, limping over and handing the counselor her racquet. "You can take my place. It'll be fun."

◆ ◆ ◆

Brooke ate her lunch as fast as she could, barely hearing the other girls' chatter. The youngers were scheduled for their next riding lesson in a little while, and Brooke really wanted to spend some quality time with Foxy before everyone else got to the barn. Besides, she figured the pony could use some extra grooming. Even though Brooke had curried and brushed her several times since their arrival, Foxy still looked a little scruffy next to the pampered horses all around her.

The barn was quiet when Brooke entered. Only a few horses were in their stalls waiting to be ridden instead of out in the pastures. Robin, Abby, and the other campers were still at lunch. None of the adult boarders were around, and Felicia had already finished her morning chores and gone home. Brooke was glad—she'd felt much better after her private time with Foxy the day before, and since it seemed she wouldn't be allowed to repeat their solo ride, this would have to do.

Foxy was outside in her paddock when Brooke reached her stall, but the mare came inside at Brooke's whistle.

"Good girl," Brooke said, rubbing her pony's nose. "Ready for your beauty treatments?"

Foxy snorted, which Brooke decided to take as a yes. She led Foxy out of the stall, clipped her into the nearest set of crossties, and went to work. She'd finished picking out Foxy's hooves and was working on a muddy spot with a rubber curry when Paige entered.

"Hey," Paige said, wandering over with her usual friendly smile. "I thought you might be out here. Want some company?"

Brooke already had all the company she wanted in Foxy. But it didn't seem polite to say so, so instead she said, "Sure. I was just giving Foxy a good grooming." She shot the other girl a shy sidelong look. "Your horses are all so sleek and shiny, it sort of inspired me."

"Aw, thanks." Paige looked pleased by the compliment. "I can't take all the credit, though. Snow is on full care at my home barn, and the grooms do an amazing job keeping her clipped and pulled and clean." Suddenly her eyes lit up. "Hey, I have an idea. Want to pull Foxy's mane? I could help you—I'm actually pretty good at it."

"Pull her mane?" Brooke glanced from Foxy, with her long, wild mane, to the horses in the nearest stalls. All of their manes were tidy and short. Brooke liked the look; she'd thought about pulling Foxy's mane once about a year earlier after reading a how-to site on the Internet. But somehow she'd never gotten around to it.

"Yeah." Paige sounded enthusiastic. "She'd look adorable with a pulled mane! Like the world's cutest show pony."

That made up Brooke's mind. Foxy might not always act like she belonged here, but this way at least maybe she'd look the part.

"Sure," Brooke said. "Thanks. That would be great. How do we start?"

"First let's brush out her mane and get it all lying on the right side of her neck," Paige said, digging into Brooke's grooming bucket for a big plastic comb.

That part went pretty well. Foxy didn't seem to mind being fussed over. She didn't even object when Paige fetched a spray bottle from the tack room and squirted the mane with water to make it lie flat.

"Okay," Paige said, finally seeming satisfied. "Now

we'll start pulling." She'd grabbed a little metal comb from the tack room while she was in there, which she now used to separate out a small section of mane. "You hold the comb like this and wrap the longest ends around it. See? Then give it a sharp yank, like this."

She did just that, pulling out some of the mane hairs with the comb. Foxy jerked her head up and took a step backward. "Easy, girl," Brooke said, rubbing the pony's neck. "Did that hurt?"

"It doesn't hurt them," Paige said, flipping her own red hair out of the way, over her shoulder. "Not any more than it hurts them for you to grab a handful of mane to steady yourself while you're riding." She shrugged. "Foxy's probably just not used to the feeling, that's all. She'll get over it."

But she didn't. With each yank of the pulling comb, the mare got more agitated. Brooke stood at her head, trying to soothe her with words and pats. Finally, though, Foxy had had enough. As Paige pulled another cluster of hairs out, the mare jerked her head up and back. The crossties snapped, and Foxy was loose.

"Whoa!" Brooke cried, alarmed. "Easy, girl."

"What's going on?" It was Hannah. She'd just arrived in the barn, with Livi right behind her.

"We were pulling Foxy's mane, and she set back and broke the ties. No biggie." Paige didn't sound that upset.

But Brooke's face was flaming. "Um, I guess she likes her mane the way it is," she quipped weakly. "It's okay, girl. . . ."

Luckily, Foxy didn't seem interested in running off. She let Brooke grab her halter and lead her over to another set of ties.

"Want to try again?" Paige asked. "Maybe you could hold her while I pull or something?"

"No, that's okay." Brooke didn't meet the other girl's eye. "It'll be time for our lesson soon. We should probably just tack up."

"By the way," Robin said as Brooke and the other girls carried their dishes into the kitchen after dinner that night. "I forgot to mention, you're all welcome to use the computer in my office if you need to check e-mail or anything."

Brooke stopped short, the thought of contact with

home making her smile for the first time in hours. "Um, I'd like to do that, if it's okay," she told Robin.

Livi gave her a confused look. "Can't you just check e-mail on your phone?"

"I don't have the Internet on my phone." Brooke tried not to notice the incredulous look on the other girl's face. Hannah wrinkled her nose as if trying to figure out the concept of a phone without Internet access, and even Paige looked surprised.

"You could have asked to borrow one of our phones," she said.

"It's okay," Brooke said. "This will be easier. I'll be out in a minute." Brooke was relieved when Paige nodded and followed the other two toward the back door.

"It's down the hall, second door on the left," Robin said.

"Thanks." Brooke found her way to the office. It was a small room that seemed even smaller due to the fact that every inch of wall space was covered in framed horse show photos and racks of ribbons. In some of the photos Brooke recognized a younger Robin piloting various gorgeous horses over tall jumps. Many others featured a pretty teenager with Robin's strong chin and blue eyes. Brooke looked at the inscription beneath one of them: *Morgan Montgomery, Junior Jumper Champion, Upperville Horse Show.*

Robin's daughter. Brooke glanced at a case full of trophies that took up most of one wall. A lot of them had Morgan's name on them too. Obviously Robin's daughter had showed and won a lot before she'd gone off to college. Brooke wondered how someone like that could stand living in New York City, so far away from her old horsey life.

She spent a few more minutes looking at the pictures and trophies before remembering why she was there. Robin's computer sat on a small wooden desk that was crammed into the corner by the trophy case. Sitting down, Brooke logged on to her e-mail account. There was a short note from her mother and another from her grandparents, both wishing her well at camp. Aside from a couple of ads and a bunch of messages notifying her of new posts on the Pony Post, that was it. There was nothing from Adam.

He probably figures I won't be able to check in anyway, Brooke told herself, logging off of her account. *Maybe I'll send him an e-mail later.*

She typed in the address for the Pony Post and logged in. Then she pushed her glasses up her nose and leaned forward to scan the site. As she'd expected, there were lots of new entries. Quite a few were about her.

[MADDIE] I wonder if Brooke will be able to email us from camp?

[HALEY] I'm sure she will. It's not like she's going to camp in Siberia!

[MADDIE] lol, I know. But my friend Bridget goes to this arts camp every summer where they aren't allowed to bring any elec. stuff. Not even phones. She can only email me like once a week.

[NINA] ugh, I'd die! Anyway, hi B, if you're out there! Hope you're having a fab time at camp!

[HALEY] Ditto! Hi Brooke!

[HALEY] She & Foxy are probably having so much fun she'll forget all about us tho, lol!

[MADDIE] Never! But I hope she's having a blast!

Brooke scanned the rest of the entries, mostly just regular chitchat about what the others had been doing with their ponies. Reading her friends' cheerful words made Brooke feel both happy and weirdly sad. If only they were here with her, camp would be a whole different experience!

She couldn't help slipping into daydreams of all the fun she'd be having if the other Pony Posters were there. They'd help each other through Robin's tough riding lessons and talk late into the night in the bunkhouse. Maybe Brooke would lead her friends to that beach she and Foxy had discovered. If the cranky old lady caught them again, Nina could probably charm her into letting them stay, and then Maddie would surely have some fun ideas for games of beach tag or something, and daredevil Haley would probably convince them all to try jumping their ponies over the rocks or swimming them in the Sound. . . .

Finally Brooke blinked and snapped back to reality, not sure how much time had passed. Glancing out the tiny window just visible between a shelf full of trophies and a rack crowded with multicolored horse show ribbons, she saw that the sky was dark. Oops. A glance at her watch told Brooke it was past time for lights-out. Robin would probably be along soon to chase her off to her bunk.

Brooke was about to shut down the computer when she realized she hadn't posted a response to her friends yet. She opened a text box and typed quickly.

> [BROOKE] Hi guys! I'm here. Camp is fine so far. Foxy and I have a lot to learn! The other campers are nice. Wish u guys were here instead, tho!

She paused, reading over the last line. Once again, her mind drifted as she imagined how much fun the four of them could have here together.

But never mind. Wishes didn't move merchandise, as her stepfather liked to say. Brooke added *GTG! More later!* at the end of her entry, then pressed enter and signed off.

When she left the office, the house was dark and quiet. She tiptoed down the hall, surprised that Robin hadn't noticed she was still out and about, and not particularly wanting to alert her to that fact. As she passed an open window, voices drifted in on the evening breeze.

"I was hoping we could at least enjoy one evening before this came up again, Preston." That was Robin; she sounded kind of annoyed.

A man's voice responded: "Why put it off? You need to look at this logically."

Robin responded, but she'd lowered her voice enough so Brooke couldn't make out what she said. All she caught were the words "farm" and "big change" and "rush."

Preston's voice was louder. "Well, you can't sit on this decision forever."

"I know." Robin's voice was louder again too, and sharp—like when she reprimanded a horse that tried to nip. "But not tonight."

Realizing she was eavesdropping, if only accidentally, Brooke jumped back into motion before she heard any more. When she reached the cabin, the other girls were already in bed.

"There you are," Hannah said with a yawn. "You must have had a ton of e-mails to read."

Paige giggled. "Yeah. We were just going to send out a search party."

Brooke doubted that—if they'd really been worried about her, wouldn't they have come looking by now?—but she didn't say so. "I'm here," she said instead. "Um, listen, I was wondering something. Preston is the guy Robin mentioned before, right? Her boyfriend or something?"

"Yeah." Livi snuggled farther into her covers. "It's kind of a romantic story. Preston heard about this place from his cousin, and dropped by to see if Robin was interested in selling the farm."

"Selling the farm?" Brooke echoed.

"Uh-huh," Paige said. "He's in real estate. My stepdad knows him and says he's a real go-getter." She giggled. "Sounds dorky, right? But coming from my stepdad, it's supposed to be a compliment."

"Anyway"—Livi picked up the story again—"Robin said no to the selling thing, but when Preston asked her out she said yes."

"And the rest is history," Hannah mumbled sleepily, her dark eyes falling shut as she snuggled back under her covers. "You'll meet him tomorrow, probably. Robin said he's supposed to get here tonight. I guess he's helping out this year or something."

"Yeah, which is kind of weird, actually." Livi wrinkled her nose. "He never showed much interest in horses before."

"Hmm." Brooke was already losing interest. Whatever she'd heard, it was none of her business. So what if Robin and Preston had been arguing? Brooke's mom and stepfather argued all the time, and it was no big deal.

As the others drifted off to sleep, Brooke lay awake feeling unsettled and homesick. Seeing the nice words from her Pony Post friends had only reminded her once again how well she fit in with them—and how much she *didn't* fit in at Camp Pocomoke. She'd never be like Robin and her daughter in those pictures, holding their trophies and patting their fancy show horses. That didn't mean she couldn't learn a lot from Robin, but was it really worth it? Maybe Brooke and Foxy were wasting everyone's time, including their own, trying to fit in here. Maybe they should go back home where they were comfortable. For a second Brooke was tempted to dig her cell phone out of her cubby, call her mother, and beg to come home early.

Then she imagined telling her Pony Post friends. None of them would ever give up so quickly, would they?

The answer came into her mind immediately: *No way!*

So maybe Brooke shouldn't give up just yet either. Maybe she should stick it out, at least for another day or two. That way, nobody could say she hadn't given it a real try.

◆ CHAPTER ◆ 7

BROOKE AWOKE WITH A START THE NEXT morning when a bird burst into enthusiastic song right outside the bunkhouse window. She sat up, rubbing her eyes, and glanced around. The other beds were empty—Paige's neatly made, Livi's a complete mess, and Hannah's somewhere in between. Brooke checked her watch and saw that she was late for breakfast.

"Thanks for waking me, guys," she muttered as she climbed out of bed.

She dressed quickly, not bothering to shower, and rushed to the main house. There was barely time to choke down half a piece of toast and a few gulps of orange juice before Robin was shooing them off to the barn for their morning lesson.

As she pulled Foxy out of her stall, Brooke was feeling rushed and sleepy and generally out of sorts. The pony seemed to pick up on her mood, spooking at the click of the crosstie being clipped on and generally being antsy and difficult all during grooming and tacking.

Robin wasn't in the ring yet when the girls entered. The other three mounted their horses, barely pausing in their conversation as they did so.

Finally it was Brooke's turn at the mounting block. But Foxy stepped to the side before her rider could put her foot in the stirrup. Brooke climbed down and led her around for another try, but the pony did the same thing.

"Quit it, would you?" Brooke exclaimed, yanking on the reins to try to stop Foxy from moving off a third time.

"Easy, Brooke." Robin had hurried into the ring at that very moment. "It won't help to lose patience with her. Here, let's try it again. . . ."

"Thanks." Brooke noticed that a man had also appeared and was leaning on the rail, watching. He was around

Robin's age or maybe a little younger, tall and well-groomed in khaki pants and a polo shirt.

Robin noticed her looking. "Brooke, that's Preston," she said. "He'll be helping out with some of our activities this week. Preston, this is Brooke Rhodes."

"Hello, Brooke," Preston said with a brief smile.

"Hi." Brooke felt self-conscious with the man watching, but with Robin holding Foxy's head, the mare finally stood still long enough for Brooke to mount.

However, the lesson only went downhill from there.

"Quiet legs, Brooke," Robin called from the center of the ring as Foxy jumped into a canter when Brooke was trying to get her to trot in a circle. "But Foxy is bending better today—nice work."

Brooke hardly heard the compliment. Foxy had just spurted forward again, even though Brooke was sure she hadn't moved her legs at all.

"Watch it!" Livi exclaimed, pulling her horse to a halt just in time to avoid a collision.

"Sorry," Brooke muttered, wrestling Foxy into a circle to slow her down. But the mare didn't settle until they started some gymnastic exercises over low jumps, which Foxy actually seemed to enjoy. By then, however, Brooke's own mood had soured beyond repair.

"Nice riding, everyone," Robin said after the girls had all gone through the exercise for the third or fourth time. "We'll quit there."

"Really?" Paige sounded disappointed. "I was hoping we'd finally do some higher jumps today."

"It's not about the height of the jumps, Paige," Robin said.

She started lecturing about basics and the foundations of riding, but Brooke wasn't really listening. Would the other girls already be jumping three-foot courses if she wasn't here? The thought made her wince.

As the whole group left the ring, Robin checked her watch. "Abby's going to be late today, so you guys are on your own while I teach the olders' lesson," she said. "How about if you take a walk to the farm stand after you put your horses away? It would be nice to have some fresh peaches for dessert."

"You mean the farm stand up the road where that cute

high school boy works?" Livi brightened. "I'm in!"

"Me too," Hannah and Paige chorused.

Brooke didn't say anything until after all the horses were untacked, groomed, and turned out into the pasture. As the other girls set out for the driveway, she hung back.

"I think I'll skip the walk," she called. "I didn't have time for a shower this morning, and I thought I'd take one now."

"Are you sure?" Paige asked. "The guy who works there is really cute!"

"Let her stay." Hannah adjusted her ponytail and wet her lips. "I don't need any more competition."

Livi laughed. "Catch you later, Brooke."

Half an hour later, Brooke toweled off her hair as she stepped out of the steamy bunkhouse bathroom. Her long, hot shower had actually improved her mood a little—and abruptly running out of hot water at the end had finally chased away the last of her lingering sleepiness.

As she wandered over to her bunk in search of clean

clothes, she heard raised voices drifting in from outside.

It was Robin and Preston. Once again they were involved in a heated discussion, this time in what they probably thought was a private spot behind the barn. Didn't the two of them ever do anything but argue? Brooke froze, clutching her towel and wishing they'd move on.

"And if you're going to sell, this is the time to do it," Preston was saying forcefully. "The offer won't be there forever."

Brooke flashed back to what the girls had told her the night before—that Preston had wanted to help Robin sell the farm. But that had happened ages ago, and Robin had said no, hadn't she?

"I'm just not ready to commit," Robin said. "Your friend might be on a tight schedule, but this is my home."

"I know, I know. But you've been complaining about being short on funds, and the developer really wants to move on this—there's a huge demand for high-end condos in this area, and most of the landowners won't budge. If you're the first one to jump on this offer, you can pretty much write your own ticket."

Brooke gasped, almost dropping her towel. Was Preston seriously suggesting that Robin sell the farm so that someone could tear it down and build a bunch of ugly condos?

"And I told you, I don't have time for this right now, Preston." Robin's voice was clipped. "Maybe in a few weeks, after camp is over . . ."

"Won't you at least talk to the man before then?" Preston sounded frustrated, but his next words were gentler. "I know it's hard to part with this place, but think about it, Robin. You'd clear more than enough to move anywhere you like. You could stop worrying about money. You wouldn't even have to work if you didn't want to, never mind running yourself ragged like you've been doing since your daughter moved out."

"I'm fine. I'm used to hard work."

"I know. But wouldn't it be nice to take a break, try something different for a while? Maybe the two of us could move to New York City, near your daughter. Won't you promise me you'll at least consider this deal? Consider what it could mean for you—for us?"

Robin didn't answer for a moment. "Fine, okay. I'll consider it. But not right now. I'm already late for the olders' lesson."

The next thing Brooke heard was footsteps hurrying away. She sank onto her bed, not caring that she was dripping all over her sheets as she tried to take in what she'd just heard. Her eyes filled with tears as she imagined bulldozers knocking down the barn and backhoes digging up the lush pastures. This land, this whole part of the peninsula, was so special, so wild and beautiful and unspoiled. A bunch of condos would change that forever. Brooke couldn't bear the thought. Robin wouldn't actually sell Pocomoke Stables to Preston's developer friend—would she?

On Thursday morning Brooke awoke from restless, disturbing dreams in which skyscrapers kept sprouting up on Assateague Island until the ponies were all crowded out into the sea. She hadn't said a word to anyone about what she'd overheard the day before, though she couldn't stop thinking about it. Maybe she wasn't having as much fun at Camp Pocomoke as she'd expected, but it was still horrible to think about a place like this being plowed under.

She remained distracted as she tacked up for the morning lesson. "Hey, is that a new trend?" Hannah called from the next set of crossties.

"Huh?" Brooke blinked at the other girl.

Hannah grinned and waved a hand toward Foxy. "Foxy's halter. You're putting it on inside out."

"Oops." Brooke realized she was right. She quickly fixed the halter, frowning at it.

Paige was walking by on her way to the tack room, but she stopped and stared at Brooke. "Are you okay? You seem kind of—I don't know, bummed out today."

"Yeah," Livi said, coming up behind Paige. "You hardly said a word at breakfast."

Brooke wasn't sure how Livi could tell, since she and the other two had spent the entire meal blabbing about shopping and haircuts and other boring topics. "I'm just a little tired, I guess." Brooke reached for a bottle of fly spray and aimed it at Foxy's side.

"Stop!" Paige cried, grabbing the bottle out of Brooke's hand. "What are you doing?"

"What do you mean?" Brooke said with a flash of irritation. "Robin said we should all share the fly spray, and I need it for Foxy—the blackflies ate her alive yesterday."

"Yeah, but this isn't fly spray." Paige shook the bottle at her. "It's Show Sheen. If you spray it all over her, your saddle will slide right off next time you ride!"

"Plus, it won't do a thing for the flies," Livi put in.

"Oops," Brooke said again, feeling flustered. "Sorry about that. I'm just distracted because of what Preston . . . um, I mean . . ." She stopped, realizing she'd almost blurted out what she'd overheard.

"Preston what?" Hannah's gaze was sharp and curious as she dropped her brush and came closer. "What is it, Brooke? What did Preston do?"

Livi gasped. "I know! Is he planning to propose to Robin?" She clapped her hands. "I knew it! That must be why he's hanging around so much this week. It's about time—they've been dating forever!"

"No, nothing like that," Brooke said. "I mean, not that I know of. I mean . . ."

Glancing around at the three girls, she knew she wasn't

going to be able to resist their voracious appetite for gossip. Besides, why not tell them the truth? They obviously had a lot of happy memories of this place. Maybe they could figure out how to change Robin's mind if she really was thinking about selling.

"It's something I heard yesterday," Brooke said. "Robin and Preston were talking—they didn't know I was nearby. Preston was trying to talk her into selling Pocomoke Stables to some developer friend of his who wants to build condos here."

She held her breath, waiting for the other girls to explode with outrage and dismay. Instead, they exchanged a puzzled glance.

Then Hannah shrugged. "Are you sure you heard them right?"

"Yeah, Preston's always talking about some boring real estate deal or other," Livi added. "You probably misunderstood."

Paige nodded. "Robin would never sell Pocomoke Stables. She's owned it for like twenty years—she and her husband built the place together before he died."

Brooke frowned. "I know what I heard. They were definitely talking about selling Pocomoke!"

The others traded another look. "Okay, if you say so." Hannah sounded skeptical. "It's just, we know Robin pretty well. . . ."

"So are you calling me a liar? I know what I heard!" Brooke clenched her fists at her sides, suddenly tired of this whole conversation. Exhausted, actually. What did she care if they believed her? She was never coming back here again if she could help it anyway. So what if their precious camp got plowed under? Their rich parents would probably just buy some of the fancy condos that replaced it!

"Brooke, listen." Paige's tone was reasonable, but Brooke wasn't listening. She'd had enough.

Unclipping Foxy from the crossties, Brooke snapped on a lead rope with shaking hands and gave a tug. The pony, who had been half asleep, awoke with a start and allowed herself to be dragged down the aisle.

"Brooke, hang on." Paige hurried after her. "We didn't mean to make you mad."

Brooke didn't respond. As soon as she got outside, she vaulted onto Foxy's bare back.

"Brooke!" This time Paige sounded alarmed. "Stop! If you ride off alone again, Robin will—"

The clatter of Foxy's hooves on the cobblestones drowned out the rest. Brooke didn't look back as she headed for the grass, then turned and nudged her pony into a trot. So what if she got in trouble again? Good! Maybe Robin would be so angry, she'd send her home. Then Brooke wouldn't have to spend another moment worrying about this stupid place.

"Come on, Foxy," she whispered, giving a cluck and a squeeze to send the mare into a canter. "Let's get out of here."

◆ CHAPTER ◆
8

AS SOON AS SHE WAS OUT OF SIGHT OF THE stable, Brooke slowed Foxy to a walk. Her anger had already faded, and she had the uncomfortable feeling that she might have overreacted. The pony ambled along, circling the soybean field and heading for the woods. It was a beautiful summer day and birds were everywhere, their cheerful songs adding the top note to the lazy drone of insects. Brooke breathed in the familiar scents of pine and marsh and sun-warmed dirt. Closing her eyes, she enjoyed the feel of the pony's muscles working beneath her. For a second she could imagine they really were on Assateague, alone except for the wildlife and the sea breeze.

Then that dream shoved back into her memory, the hideous skyscrapers pushing up through the sand to ruin the landscape. Brooke's eyes flew open, and she shuddered. She couldn't believe the other girls hadn't believed what she'd told them. They'd be sorry when the first bulldozers came crashing into their beloved Camp Pocomoke!

But again her anger faded quickly, this time leaving her feeling sad. As they entered the woods, every tree and bird and squirrel she saw seemed so beautiful and alive that Brooke couldn't stand the thought that they might soon be destroyed or displaced just so a bunch of rich city people could buy part of what used to be the country.

As soon as they emerged on the far side of the woods, Brooke turned Foxy to the right, staying on the near side of the dirt road that ran along the edge of the trees. She guessed that was the line that divided the farm she'd just crossed from Miss Alice's property, and she planned to stay on the good side of it. She definitely didn't want to get yelled at again.

"Hey! You there, girl and pony!"

Brooke tensed. Glancing over her shoulder, she saw Miss Alice hurrying up the hill, waving her cane. Uh-oh.

Had she guessed wrong? Was she trespassing again after all?

"Sorry!" she called. "We're leaving."

"No, wait. Come here," the old woman ordered.

Brooke almost ignored her and turned Foxy back into the woods. But the old woman was alone this time, and the way she was climbing heedlessly over the rocks and sand in her clunky shoes made Brooke worry that she'd stumble and break a hip. Besides, now that she took another look, Miss Alice didn't look angry. In fact, she actually appeared to be smiling.

Biting her lip, Brooke rode toward the woman. They met at the edge of the dirt road. Miss Alice was huffing and puffing, but her expression was pleasant.

"Good, you came back," she said. "I was afraid you wouldn't after last time."

"Um . . ." Brooke had no idea what to say to that.

Foxy stretched her nose toward Miss Alice and snuffled curiously at her. Brooke was afraid the old woman would be annoyed, but Miss Alice's smile widened as she rubbed the pony's velvety muzzle.

"Natalie scolded me all afternoon about that, you know,"

she told Brooke. "Said I was a proper ogre. Don't tell her, but she may have been right." She leaned a little closer and winked at Brooke.

"No, it's fine," Brooke said. "I know better than to ride anywhere I don't have permission. My parents made me ask all the neighbors before I ever rode Foxy off our own land."

"They sound like good parents," the old woman said. "I'm Alice Foster, by the way. But you can call me Miss Alice—everyone does."

"I'm Brooke. Brooke Rhodes. I'm from Camp Pocomoke."

"That's what I figured." Miss Alice gave Foxy another pat. "You know, I used to ride as a girl. Always found trotting around a ring a bit stifling, though." She let out a short bark of laughter. "But back then, proper young ladies didn't go gallivanting off bareback over the countryside." She looked up at Brooke. "You say this girl's a Chincoteague pony, eh? Do you young people still read *Misty of Chincoteague*?"

"Yes!" Brooke blurted out in surprise. "It's my favorite book—it's the reason I wanted a Chincoteague pony of my own."

"Good, good." Miss Alice seemed pleased. "I read it the very first year it was published. After that, I secretly dreamed of getting myself a pony just like Misty and exploring the shores and inlets to my heart's content. Never happened, of course." A shadow of sadness crossed her wrinkled face. "But when I saw you riding toward me the other day, I wondered if I'd finally lost my mind and my old dreams were coming to life!"

Brooke relaxed. Suddenly Miss Alice didn't seem scary at all anymore. She was just a grown-up pony-crazy girl!

"In any case, I'm sorry for snapping at you before," the old woman said.

"It's okay," Brooke replied.

"No it's not. But I do have an excuse." Miss Alice picked a leaf out of Foxy's forelock. "My nephew and his daughters moved back to Maryland last month. They're living in my guest cottage, and I guess I'm having a little trouble adjusting. Been a long time since I had to share my place with anyone else."

Again, Brooke thought the old woman's eyes looked

sad for a moment. And no wonder. This area was wild and beautiful, but it had to be a little lonely living out here all alone for so long.

"Was that one of your nephew's daughters who was with you last time?" Brooke asked. "She seemed interested in ponies, too."

"That was Natalie, yes. Sixteen and so grown-up!" Miss Alice looked proud. "Now, how are you liking Camp Pocomoke?"

Brooke shrugged. "It's okay, I guess."

"Just okay?" Miss Alice raised an eyebrow. "I haven't seen much of Robin Montgomery in a while, but she always seemed capable enough to me. Shame, that lovely husband of hers dying so young. Cancer, you know."

"Oh." Brooke cleared her throat. "Yeah, Robin's great. And the camp is nice, too. It's just . . ." She hesitated, shooting the old woman a sidelong look. Brooke wasn't normally the type of person to open up to someone after just meeting her. Somehow, though, after hearing Miss Alice's story, Brooke had the feeling the old woman might understand what she was going through, at least a little.

"I'm just not sure Foxy and I fit in there with all those fancy horses and riders."

"Hmm." Miss Alice shrugged her thin shoulders. "Your Foxy looks fancy enough to me. Does that mean you won't be coming back next summer?"

"Maybe nobody will be coming back next summer," Brooke blurted out before she realized what she was saying. At Miss Alice's surprised look, she suddenly found herself telling her everything she'd heard about the potential real estate deal.

By the end, Miss Alice looked alarmed. "This simply won't do," she exclaimed, tapping her cane firmly on the ground. "Robin can't sell her farm! Once the first developer starts knocking down trees and building condos and shopping centers and parking lots, it's only a matter of time until the whole way of life around here is ruined! It's happened lots of other places, and I can't bear to see it happen here."

"I know." Brooke looked around at the beautiful scenery surrounding them. "But what can we do about it? It's Robin's decision, I guess. And like my stepfather always says, money talks."

"But you don't have to listen!" Miss Alice exclaimed. "Look here, young lady. If you care about Pocomoke Stables, or even just about wild places like the one where your pony came from, you need to do something to stop this!"

Brooke was taken aback by her sudden fierceness. "Um, I would if I could. But I'm just a kid."

"Paul and Maureen Beebe were just kids, too." Miss Alice leaned closer, gazing up into Brooke's eyes. "And look at all they did!" Suddenly she stepped back, looking tired. "Oh, listen to me railing on. I should get home before Dan sends out a search party. But think about what I've said, all right?" She started to turn away, then paused and glanced back over her shoulder. "And by the way, you and Foxy are welcome to trespass here anytime."

When Brooke got back to the barn, Robin was nowhere in sight. But Paige, Livi, and Hannah were waiting for her.

"We covered for you," Hannah announced.

Livi nodded. "We told Robin you were taking a nap." She giggled. "Luckily, she didn't notice Foxy was missing too, or we'd have had a lot of explaining to do."

Brooke blinked at them, confused. "Um, okay."

"We're sorry for not believing you earlier," Paige went on. "Hannah spied on Preston and found out you were totally right."

Hannah tugged on her glossy dark ponytail. "Totally," she agreed. "I followed him around all stealthy, like one of the PIs my dad hires sometimes."

"PIs?" Brooke was feeling more and more confused. She slid down from Foxy's back and led her into the barn.

The other girls followed. "Private investigators," Hannah explained. "My dad's a lawyer, and he hires them sometimes when his clients— Oh, never mind!" She shook her head impatiently. "The point is, I heard Preston call up somebody and start talking about how he was working on Robin, trying to convince her to sell this place."

Paige clenched her fists. "I can't believe it! What a jerk. If he really cared about Robin, he'd want to her be happy. And how could she ever be happy anywhere else but here?"

"Yeah." Livi frowned, then sighed. "And I mean, what are we going to do without this place?"

"I know, right?" Paige said, while Hannah just looked sad.

Brooke didn't say anything as she led Foxy into her stall. The other girls really did love this place, and no wonder. Just from listening to their chatter over the past few days, Brooke knew they had tons of happy memories of Pocomoke Stables. For a second that made her feel more like an outsider than ever.

"We never would have met without this place," Paige exclaimed.

Livi grabbed her in a hug. "Yeah. And I totally can't imagine not being friends with you guys."

"And poor Lauren." Hannah sniffled, joining the others' hug. "She won't even get one last summer here!"

Brooke found herself thinking about the Pony Post. She couldn't imagine not being friends with Maddie, Haley, and Nina, either.

Maybe these girls aren't so different from me after all, Brooke thought as she hung Foxy's halter on the hook outside her stall.

"So what are you going to do about it?" she asked, still thinking about her own friends. Maddie had recently come up with all kinds of wild plans to keep her riding instructor from selling her favorite pony. Maybe these girls could do the same kind of thing to save Pocomoke Stables.

"Do about what?" Livi said, stepping back from the group hug.

Hannah shrugged. "What *can* we do?"

"Yeah." Paige sighed. "We just have to accept it if it happens, I guess. But it won't be easy."

Brooke's jaw dropped. It was tearing her up to imagine the fate of this pristine corner of the Eastern Shore if Robin sold out to that developer—and it had to be even worse for the other girls with all their special memories.

"Are you serious?" she blurted out. "You can't just let it happen. You have to find a way to save this place!"

• CHAPTER •

THAT NIGHT, BROOKE HAD JUST CRAWLED into her sleeping bag when there was a tap on the bunkhouse door. A second later Robin stuck her head in.

"Lights out," she said, flipping the switch off. "Sleep tight, girls. I'll see you bright and early."

"'Night," all four girls chorused.

As soon as the door shut, Hannah sat up and flung away her covers. "Okay," she said briskly. "Let's talk."

"Yeah." Paige rolled onto her side and propped her head on her hand. "Brooke's right. We can't just sit back and let this happen."

"Totally," Livi agreed.

This was the first chance they'd had to talk in private since Brooke's return to the barn. Felicia had come along to ask for help dragging the ring right after that, and then Abby had turned up to take the girls to play golf. By the time they got back it was already time to feed the horses, and after dinner Robin had showed the whole group, youngers and olders alike, some training videos.

"Right. So we need a plan," Hannah said. "Brooke?"

"Huh?" Brooke sat up too. Even in the dim moonlight filtering in through the windows, she could see that the other three girls were staring at her.

"Do you have any ideas about what to do?" Paige asked.

"Me? Um . . ." Brooke realized they were expecting her to take charge of this meeting. Had she just gone from being an outsider to being the group leader? It was a weird thought. "I guess we should just all come up with ideas and figure out the best ones."

"What kind of ideas?" Livi looked blank.

Brooke shrugged. "Ways to change Robin's mind."

"I have an idea," Paige said tentatively. "We could talk to the olders and see what they think."

Hannah wrinkled her nose. "That's not a plan. Brooke means something *we* can do, like convince Robin there's a secret diamond mine in the back pasture so she won't want to sell."

Paige laughed. "Or how about we hire a sorcerer to put an amnesia spell on Preston so he forgets all about his horrible deal?"

"Yeah, right." Livi giggled. "If we're going to hire a sorcerer, we should just have him poof up enough cash so Robin doesn't *need* Preston's friend's money!"

Brooke laughed, but Hannah sighed and rolled her eyes. "This is pointless," she announced, swinging her long legs over the edge of her bunk. "I say we just go talk to Robin right now."

"Now? But we're supposed to be sleeping," Paige said.

"So what?" Hannah jammed her feet into her sandals and marched toward the door. "This is important. Robin will forgive us when she hears what we want to talk about."

Livi turned to Brooke. "What do you think?"

Brooke thought for a second. It would be awkward telling Robin they knew about the deal, especially since

Brooke would probably have to admit she'd accidentally eavesdropped on Robin and Preston. But maybe it would be worth it.

"I guess Hannah's right," she said. "I mean, we know Preston wants Robin to sell, but we don't really know if she's seriously thinking about it. It's probably better to find out so we don't waste time coming up with plans we might not even need."

Livi brightened. "That's true," she said. "Robin's probably just trying to figure out how to tell Preston no without making him mad."

"I hope so." Paige didn't sound quite as optimistic. "Okay, let's go talk to her."

Soon all four of them were hurrying across the courtyard. The moon was almost full, and the farm looked magical and dreamlike under its silvery light. But Brooke was too nervous to enjoy the scene. As they neared the house, she heard voices up ahead.

Hannah, who was in the lead, held up a hand. "Shh. Sounds like Robin's with Preston," she whispered.

The girls crept toward the tall evergreen hedge that

separated the courtyard from the back garden. "Let's try to hear if they're talking about the deal," Livi said.

"But that's eavesdropping!" Paige's eyes widened.

"Just come on." Hannah yanked her forward.

Soon the four of them were crouched behind the hedge. Through the tangle of branches, Brooke saw Robin and Preston sitting in lounge chairs, sipping from wine-glasses. Their voices were quiet, but the night was still and it was easy to hear them.

". . . and it's been a lot harder than I thought since she left," Robin was saying.

"I know." Preston sounded sympathetic. "Morgan was a big part of this place. It's not going to be the same without her."

Brooke realized they were talking about Robin's daughter. She leaned closer, holding her breath as she listened.

"I guess part of me thought she'd change her mind," Robin went on. "That after a couple of weeks in New York, she'd miss this place and come home."

"But that's not happening."

"No. She loves being in the heart of the fashion industry." Robin's voice was sad. "I have to accept that she's found her true passion, and it's not the one I thought it was."

"Wow," Livi whispered. "I knew Morgan was studying fashion design in college, but—"

"Shhh!" Paige warned.

Robin was talking again. "Morgan and I ran this place together for so long. Somehow I thought it would always be that way, you know?"

"Things change," Preston commented. "Sometimes for the better."

Robin didn't answer for a moment. Then she sighed. "It's just a lot lonelier without her here. I love running the farm, but lately the bills just seem to go up and up, and I'm feeling stretched to my limit. I never have time to ride anymore unless it's a training client or something. And I'm not getting any younger, either. I guess I'd always imagined Morgan would take over the business someday, but obviously she's not interested."

"Not everybody is cut out for this kind of life." Preston

paused and cleared his throat. "It's okay if you decide you're not cut out for it anymore either."

"I'm just not sure I can do it all myself without Morgan—or maybe I'm not sure I want to. There's no room in the budget for more staff, and I won't ask the people I have to work harder for the same pay."

"Then why not consider O'Malley's offer?" Preston urged. "It could be just what you need—a change. But you'll need to decide soon if you want to go for it."

"I know, I know." Robin sounded tired. "I suppose you're right. But I'm not going to make a decision tonight."

"Then when? O'Malley wants me to call him by the end of next week at the latest."

"That's the end of camp," Robin said. "All right. I'll make a decision by then. But let's not talk about it anymore right now, okay? Oh! And you can't say a word to the campers. I won't ruin their fun with my problems."

"Come on." Hannah tugged at Brooke's sleeve, her dark eyes sad. "I don't think we're going to talk to Robin tonight after all."

◆ ◆ ◆

Brooke was floating on her back with her eyes closed when a tinny version of a recent pop song erupted from near the pool.

She opened her eyes and saw Abby splashing toward the edge. "Is that my phone?" the counselor said. "Excuse me a sec."

Abby had driven Brooke and her bunkmates to the neighboring estate for a swim. For a while she'd tried to interest them in a game of Marco Polo or something, but it was an extra-hot morning and nobody was really in the mood. The girls had spent the previous hour tromping around a fallow field on a neighboring farm while Robin pointed out toxic plants and other hazards that would need to be rectified to make it safe pasture for horses. By the end of the hour, Brooke and the others were sweaty and exhausted.

"Good, she's gone." Paige swam over to where Brooke was floating. "Let's talk."

A few feet away, Livi was stretched out on an inflatable raft, working on her tan. She turned her head and squinted at Paige. "What's to talk about? You heard Robin last night. She's tired of running this place and being poor."

Brooke nodded. It was still hard to believe how completely discouraged Robin had sounded while talking to Preston. She'd seemed like a whole different person from the one she was most of the time. For instance, during the girls' horsemanship lesson earlier, Robin had been the only one who'd seemed at all enthusiastic about wandering around that hot field, looking at plants. Was that all a big act? Was Robin secretly wishing the whole time that she was in New York with her daughter, with no feed bills to pay or stalls to clean or campers to teach?

Hannah had been reading a magazine on a floating chair nearby, and paddled closer to join the conversation. "Seriously, guys. I mean, it's one thing to help Robin if she still wants to be here. She shot a cautious look toward Abby, who had her back to the pool. "But if she's not having fun, or even making enough money to live on . . ."

Brooke sighed. "There's not much we can do."

"More bend, Brooke! Use your legs—good!" Robin called from the center of the ring.

Brooke turned Foxy toward the first jump in the line

Robin had set up along one long side. The pony's ears pricked toward it, and she surged forward.

"Easy, girl," Brooke murmured, half halting the way they'd practiced during flatwork. Foxy responded and slowed, meeting the jump just right and soaring over easily.

The second obstacle in the line went just as well, and Brooke was grinning as she pulled up. She gave Foxy a pat and walked her toward the others.

"Excellent," Robin said with a smile. "Good riding, Brooke. Livi? You and Royal are up."

As Livi rode forward, Brooke stopped beside Paige and Hannah. "She's actually a good little jumper," Paige said. "You should try taking her in a show sometime."

"I'm not sure we're quite ready for that," Brooke said with a smile. "But maybe some— Oh!" She gasped as Livi's horse, who had been trotting steadily toward the first fence in the line, suddenly ducked violently to one side.

"Hang on!" Hannah shouted.

But Livi was already tumbling off the side of her horse. She landed on her rear end, and Royal took off for the far end of the ring, his tail flagging.

Robin hurried toward Livi, who was already climbing to her feet. "I'm okay," Livi called, leaning forward and resting her hands on her knees. "Knocked the breath out of me, that's all."

Brooke realized she'd been holding her own breath. She let it out, then pushed her glasses up and glanced over at Paige and Hannah. "Wow, that was scary," she said. "It must really hurt to fall off such a tall horse!"

Hannah rolled her eyes. "Livi's used to it. Royal used to run out all the time last summer, but I thought they'd fixed that."

Robin checked on Livi, then caught the big bay gelding, who was already losing interest in running around. "Why don't I get on for a moment while you catch your breath," Robin told Livi, already adjusting the stirrups on Royal's saddle. "Royal's been a little ornery today, and he could probably use some extra schooling."

"Uh-oh, Royal, you're in trouble now!" Paige called out with a grin.

Robin swung into the saddle and sent Royal forward at a walk. "I've never seen Robin ride before," Brooke commented to the girls, including Livi, who'd wandered over to stand by the other horses.

"Really? She's amazing," Livi said. "She's, like, the only reason I can jump Royal at all. She schooled him practically every day last summer—I'd only had him a month or so then, and he was pretty green."

After that they all stayed quiet as Robin rode Royal around in a big circle, first at a trot and then at a canter. At first the big bay's ears were back and his neck was tense. But within minutes Brooke could actually see him soften, his stride lengthening and his neck arching elegantly as he accepted the bit.

Finally Robin turned him toward the line of jumps. Royal slowed down when he noticed where they were headed. Brooke couldn't quite tell what Robin did, but suddenly the horse's pace steadied and he sailed over the two jumps.

Robin didn't stop there, turning Royal toward another line of higher jumps nearby. This time the horse didn't hesitate, cantering over those jumps easily as well.

When Robin pulled up near the girls, she was grinning from ear to ear. "Who's a naughty boy now?" she cooed, reaching forward to rub Royal's neck with both hands. "Not you, Royal." She winked at Livi. "Ready to give it another try?"

Soon Royal's owner was back in the saddle. Brooke held her breath as Livi aimed the horse at the jump.

"More leg, more leg!" Robin called. "Okay, a little too much—half halt! Good!"

"Go, Livi!" Paige cheered as Royal cleared the jumps.

Robin had the pair do the line once more, then hurried over to give Royal a treat and Livi a pat on the leg. "There, how'd that feel?" the instructor asked with a smile. "He really is a good boy—he just needs a confident ride to feel confident himself. And that time you gave him one! Well done."

"Thanks." Livi looked happy as she patted her horse.

"Wow, Robin really is good," Brooke whispered to Paige.

"Yeah." Paige bit her lip. "It's so obvious she loves horses and riding and teaching so much. How can she even think about giving it all up and moving to the city?"

◆ CHAPTER ◆ 10

THAT NIGHT, BROOKE PUSHED HER CHAIR back from the dinner table. "May I be excused?" she asked Robin. "I was hoping to check my e-mail again, if that's okay."

Robin looked up from her plate. "Sure, go ahead. Leave the computer on when you're finished—I need to pay some bills later."

"Okay." Brooke hurried down the hall to the office. She paused in the doorway, studying the walls and their pictorial story of Robin's life with horses. After watching Robin with Royal earlier, Brooke and the others had been unanimous: they couldn't give up yet. Maybe Robin thought she was ready for an easier life. But watching her ride, Brooke knew she'd regret it if she gave up horses. Every chance they'd had all day, the girls had tried to think of ideas to convince Robin of that. So far, though, they'd come up blank. Just about the only decision they'd made was to let the older campers know what was happening, though there hadn't been a chance to do so yet.

Logging on to her e-mail account, Brooke found a couple more notes from her mother, a short one from the twins, and a mass-mailed party invitation from a girl at school. Still nothing from Adam. She opened a new blank e-mail and started typing.

> Hey! It's me. Camp is good so far.
> What's going on at home? How's swim
> team? See u soon!
> B.

She hesitated briefly, then added Adam's address and hit send. There. At least that way he'd know she was checking e-mail at camp. If he wanted to write back, he would. If not, well, she wasn't going to worry about it. At least not right now.

Soon she was on the Pony Post site. She was scanning the entries when she saw a new one pop up at the bottom of the page:

> [HALEY] Hi all! Just checking in. Wings and I had a good ride today. My brothers cut down a big tree to make a dirt bike trail, and I turned part of it into a rly cool XC jump. Wings loved it! Will get pix soon. What's up w/ all of you?

Haley was on the site right now too! Brooke quickly opened a text box.

> [BROOKE] Hi, I'm here too!

She hit enter, then waited. A moment later Haley posted again.

[HALEY] HI!!!!!! How's camp? Are you having the best time ever?

[BROOKE] Sort of. I mean sort of? At 1st I wasn't sure I was going to like it here.

[HALEY] What do u mean?

[BROOKE] The other girls are much better riders than me. They all have big fancy show horses.

[HALEY] Ooooooh! :-P Are they snobby?

[BROOKE] I thought they were. But they're not. They're actually rly nice. I just needed to get to know them, I guess.

[HALEY] So u are all friends now?

[BROOKE] Yeh. But we have a BIG problem . . .

She typed as fast as she could, telling Haley the whole story. When she finished, she sat back. It wasn't long before another entry popped up.

[HALEY] Wowowow. That's wild!
What r u going to do?

[BROOKE] Not sure. I was hoping u
might have some ideas, lol.

[HALEY] Hmm. U don't have much time if Robin
has to give an answer by next wk. So be sure
whatever u decide to do makes sense. No
wacky plans like some of Maddie's, lol! (Don't kill
me when u read this, Mads! U know I love u!)

[BROOKE] Haha, no, I get it.
Sooooo . . . any brilliant ideas?

Brooke felt a twinge of hope as she hit enter. Haley was one of the most down-to-earth, practical people

Brooke knew. If anyone could come up with a way to save Pocomoke Stables, it was her.

Suddenly the door flew open, and Brooke's bunkmates burst into the office. "Good, you're still in here," Hannah exclaimed. "Listen, Robin and Preston just headed down to the barn for night check, so we figured this was a good time to talk."

"Yeah." Livi came in and perched on the edge of the desk, peering curiously at the computer. "Hey, what's that?" she asked, pointing at the Pony Post logo at the top of the screen.

For a second, Brooke wished she'd had time to log off before the others came in. Too late now. Another post from Haley had just popped up:

> [HALEY] What about the daughter? Can u talk to her about this? She knows her mom better than anyone.

"Um . . ." Brooke suddenly felt as shy as she had on her first day at camp. Her bunkmates were all serious show riders. Would they think the Pony Post was silly? "I met these other girls who have Chincoteague ponies—met them online, I mean—and we started a website to keep in touch and trade pictures of our ponies and stuff."

"What a cool idea!" Paige said, leaning in for a look.

"Yeah, and the graphics are gorge," Hannah added.

"Thanks." Brooke grinned with relief. The only person she'd ever told about the site outside of her parents was Adam, and he'd been about as interested in it as he was in helping clean the manure out of Foxy's pasture. "Nina's mom is an artist. She helped us design it, but we came up with the idea ourselves."

"That's awesome." Livi grabbed the mouse and scrolled down to some photos of Maddie's big trail ride. "I never heard of a site like this. How many people are on it?"

"Just four of us," Brooke said. "We're all over the country—Maddie is in California, Nina's in New Orleans, and Haley lives in Wisconsin." She waved a hand at the screen. "I was just chatting with Haley, actually. She thinks maybe we should talk to Robin's daughter or something."

Hannah's eyes widened. "Why didn't I think of that?"

she exclaimed. "I bet Morgan has no clue her mom's thinking about selling this place."

"She'd probably come straight home if she knew," Paige said, staring up at a photo of Morgan jumping a huge gray horse over an equally huge oxer. "I mean, I know Robin says she loves New York. But she loves this place even more, right?"

Livi clapped her hands. "Perfect! It's so easy—we let Morgan know what's happening and let her deal with Robin. No need to freak out."

"Or talk to the olders." Hannah grimaced. "I wasn't looking forward to listening to all of Jenna's snooty reasons why us youngers are total airheads who probably misunderstood the whole situation."

Paige giggled. "Let's e-mail Morgan right now. I'll just log on to my account—I have her addy on there."

"So you really think this will work?" Brooke stood up to let Paige take over the keyboard. She couldn't help thinking of Haley's warning—they didn't have any time to waste. It was Friday, which meant there was only one more week before Preston's deadline.

"Absolutely." Hannah sounded confident as she leaned on the back of the chair Paige was sitting on "Morgan always knows what to do. She'll take care of it."

They spent the next few minutes composing the e-mail. Brooke didn't say much, since she was the only one who didn't know Morgan. She was surprised when Paige sat back and glanced at her when she'd finished typing.

"Well?" she said. "What do you think, Brooke? How's it sound?"

Brooke leaned forward to read over the message:

> Hi Morgan! It's us, your favorite Camp Pocomoke campers! We just thought you should know that your mom really misses you. She might even sell the farm!!! (Pls don't tell her we know that tho!!!!!)
>
> Anyway, you should probably come home and talk her out of it. Who knows,

maybe you'll decide to stay! This place
is way better than NYC anyway, right?
lol!

Love,
Paige, Hannah, Livi, and Brooke

"It sounds good," Brooke said. "But maybe you shouldn't include my name. She won't know who I am, and it'll just be confusing."

"But you have to be on there," Livi insisted. "You're the main reason we even know what's going on!"

"I have an idea." Hannah leaned over Paige's shoulder. Typing with two fingers, she added an arrow pointing at Brooke's name and the words (*cool new camper*) on the other end of the arrow. "There, how's that?" she said when she finished.

Brooke blushed. "Um, fine, I guess."

"Good. Now send it—maybe she'll write back right away!" Livi said.

The four of them spent the next twenty minutes in

the office, talking and looking at Robin's pictures. Paige's e-mail account was still open, and the computer pinged several times to indicate a new message. But none of those messages were from Morgan.

Finally Livi checked her watch and sighed. "I guess she's not writing back right now," she said. "She's probably out somewhere having fun in the big city."

"Maybe she'll get back to us tomorrow." Paige grabbed the mouse to log off her e-mail. "We might as well get out of here before Robin comes in and figures out what we're doing."

"Are you sure about this?" Hannah sounded nervous.

Paige laughed. "Just get on already," she said. "I can't believe you've never ever ridden bareback before!"

"The trainer at my barn doesn't allow it," Hannah retorted with a slight frown. "And Vegas has killer withers—I'd be crazy to try it on him."

"Whatever." Livi leaned against the fence. "Foxy's the perfect shape, so stop stalling and get on."

Brooke wasn't sure she'd ever actually seen Hannah

look nervous before. But there was a furrow in Hannah's brow as she stood beside Foxy, who was wearing only her bridle. It was Saturday morning, and the girls had just finished their riding lesson. While tacking up that day, Livi had complained that it was way too hot to make their horses wear saddles and they should just ride the lesson bareback. She was only joking, but Hannah had mentioned that she'd never ridden bareback before. And not just on Vegas, which Brooke could understand—he really did have bony withers, not to mention a tendency to buck unexpectedly—but on *any* horse.

Brooke was amazed. She'd spent more time on Foxy without a saddle than with one! Some of her best memories were of exploring the countryside bareback. She hated to think that Hannah had never had the chance to experience anything like that. So she'd offered to let her ride Foxy bareback sometime if she wanted to, and while Hannah had been hesitant at first, the others had talked her into giving it a try after the lesson.

"It'll be fine," Brooke told her. "I ride Foxy bareback all the time—she's totally used to it." She glanced at Livi and Paige. "Can one of you give her a leg up? That way I can hold Foxy and make sure she stands still."

"Sure." Paige stepped forward and cupped her hands.

Hannah looked ready to protest. But instead she nodded, checked the throat strap on her helmet, and then allowed her friend to boost her up. She landed awkwardly, almost sliding off the far side before hooking one long leg around Foxy's belly and wiggling into position.

"Oh!" she exclaimed, leaning forward and clutching the pony's mane. "It feels so weird!"

"Just give yourself a second," Brooke advised. "You'll get used to it fast."

She was right. For the first few minutes, Hannah squealed and clutched at the mane every time Foxy moved a muscle. But she was a good, experienced rider, and it wasn't long before she let go of the mane and picked up the reins, walking Foxy around the lawn behind the courtyard.

"This is awesome," Hannah said after a while. "I can feel, like, every time she moves a muscle! She's really responsive to my leg and seat, too. Can I try a trot?"

"Sure," Brooke said. "Foxy's trot is super-smooth."

"Make it a short one, though," Paige put in. "We're supposed to leave for town in like twenty minutes, and we still need to change clothes."

Brooke had almost forgotten about that. As soon as the olders finished their lesson, which was going on now, the whole group was scheduled to take a trip to the nearest town, where they could do some shopping and sightseeing and then have lunch at a local restaurant.

"The olders haven't even finished yet, though. We've got time for her to try it," Brooke said. She glanced up at Hannah. "Just cluck and squeeze your legs gently, and she'll trot."

"Come on, Foxy." Hannah clucked. "Let's trot." As the pony smoothly stepped into the faster gait, Hannah grinned, automatically adjusting her position to stay with the bouncier gait. "Wheeee!"

"I'm starving!" Livi exclaimed, flopping into her chair at the diner and grabbing one of the menus the waitress had left on the table.

"Shopping is hungry work, eh?" Robin winked at

Preston, who was sitting across from her. Brooke was seated between Robin and Paige, with Livi and Hannah on Preston's side of the table. The older campers were at a table on the other side of the restaurant, laughing and chatting with Abby.

So far, the trip to town had been . . . interesting. Brooke and her bunkmates had spent the past hour or more wandering down the charming little main street, stopping into almost every shop and boutique they passed. Brooke hadn't bought anything except a package of mints, but the other girls were a different story. Watching the way they casually pulled out their own personal credit cards to buy clothes, books, makeup—even a new pair of real gold earrings, in Hannah's case—had reminded Brooke that they really did live in a whole different world from hers.

"We come to this diner every year," Paige told Brooke, handing her a menu. "The liver and onions is to die for!"

Hannah giggled. "No it's not, it's disgusting," she said. "Don't worry, Brooke. If Paige's food is too smelly, we'll make her sit at a different table."

That made everyone laugh, including Brooke. Okay,

so it had been kind of awkward to watch the others shop, knowing she couldn't afford half the stuff they took for granted. But so what? The truth was, she was having fun. In fact, despite her worries about the stable's future, she'd been having more and more fun lately. She hadn't even thought about calling her mother to come and pick her up in a couple of days.

As she was scanning the menu, the bell over the door jingled. Brooke glanced up and saw Miss Alice stepping into the restaurant. A tall, dark-haired man around Robin's age had a hand on her elbow.

"Slow down, Aunt Alice," the man said. "There's a step here."

"I know there's a step, Daniel." Miss Alice rolled her eyes, her sharp voice cutting through the noise of the busy restaurant like a car alarm. "I've only been coming to this place for the past fifty years, after all."

The man chuckled, not seeming to mind the scolding. "I'll get us a table," he said, letting go of Miss Alice's elbow and hurrying over to the hostess.

Meanwhile Miss Alice spotted Brooke. Her wrinkled

face broke into a smile, and she hurried over. "Well, well, what luck—it's the Chincoteague pony girl," she said. "How are you, Brooke? And how's the lovely Foxy?"

"I'm fine, thanks," Brooke said. "Foxy's fine too." She was aware that the other girls looked confused.

"Good, good." Miss Alice nodded to Robin. "It's been too long, Robin. Nice to see you again."

"Likewise, Miss Alice," Robin said. "I hope you're well?"

"As well as can be expected." Miss Alice's mouth twisted into a smile. Just then her nephew called her name. "Pardon me," Miss Alice said. "Enjoy your lunch."

"Who was that?" Preston asked as soon as Miss Alice was out of earshot.

"A neighbor." Robin gazed at Brooke curiously. "She seemed awfully friendly toward you, Brooke. Somehow I had the impression your meeting didn't go that well."

Brooke's cheeks went red. Robin still didn't know about her second encounter with Miss Alice. "Um, I guess it was better than I thought."

"Never mind that." Livi was watching with interest as Miss Alice and her companion took seats at a table on the opposite side of the room. "Who's the guy with her? He looks like a movie star!"

Hannah smirked. "I never knew you liked older men, Livs."

"Ha-ha, very funny!" Livi stuck out her tongue.

"I think that's her nephew," Brooke said. "Miss Alice said he and his daughters just moved in with her."

"Really? I didn't know that." Robin gave Brooke another searching look, then shrugged. "Makes sense, though. Miss Alice has two siblings, and each of them had several children if I recall correctly. She never married or had kids of her own, though—she's lived in the old family house all alone for as long as I can remember."

"Hmm." Preston turned away, clearly losing interest in the whole conversation. "Where did that waitress run off to? I'm ready to order."

◆ CHAPTER ◆ 11

"GOOD GIRL," LIVI COOED, STROKING FOXY'S nose. "See? We knew you'd behave better if your boyfriend was with you!"

Brooke grinned and gave her pony a pat. She and her bunkmates were in Foxy's paddock. A lead rope was clipped to the mare's halter and Brooke was holding it while Paige pulled Foxy's mane. Meanwhile Hannah and Livi were feeding treats over the fence to Gideon, the big bay gelding in the paddock next door. That kept him near the fence, which meant Foxy stayed more interested in him than in what the girls were doing.

"You know, I never even noticed Foxy was falling in

love with Gideon," Brooke said with a laugh. "It makes sense, though. He's the same color as her favorite draft."

"Draft?" Paige yanked another few hairs out, then glanced at Brooke. "What do you mean?"

"The neighbors behind us have a big farm where they keep some retired draft horses," Brooke explained. "They're right across the fence from Foxy's pasture. It's great, because that way Foxy feels like she's not all alone."

Livi nodded. "Robin always says horses are herd animals."

Just then a buzz came from Paige's pocket. "Oops, there's my phone." She pulled it out and gasped. "It's an e-mail from Morgan!"

Suddenly everyone, including Brooke, was much less interested in Foxy and her half-pulled mane. "What's it say?" Hannah demanded.

"Give me a sec. . . ." Paige hit a button and scanned the message. Her face fell. "See for yourself," she said, holding out the phone so Brooke and the others could read the e-mail.

Hi gang—it was great to hear from you! Hope you're having fun at camp. Thanks for being concerned about Mom, but you know her well enough to know that she can take care of herself. If she's thinking of selling (and if she is, I haven't heard about it), she's probably got a good reason.

Sorry I won't get to see you guys this summer. But things are going great here in the city. I love my new job as a design assistant! I never thought I'd find something I loved even more than horses, but I did. Giving up riding (at least for now) is worth it to make fashion my career. But I hope we can still be friends even if I'm not riding anymore—and even if it's long-distance!

Keep in touch,

Morgan

"Oh." Hannah's voice was flat. "Okay, I guess that's that."

Brooke bit her lip. "Do you want to write back and explain more?" she asked. "Maybe she didn't think we were serious."

"I don't think it'll help." Paige slipped her phone back in her pocket. "Morgan always says it like it is. She doesn't want to come home, and she's not into horses anymore."

"Yeah," Livi said. "It sounds like she doesn't even believe us."

She, Paige, and Hannah looked so dejected that Brooke could hardly stand it. "Well, we still can't give up," she insisted. "So the Morgan plan was a bust. Who's got another idea?"

Hannah sighed loudly, digging another treat out of her bag for Gideon. "I don't know. We only have a week."

"*Less* than a week," Paige pointed out. "The final show's on Friday, and then we leave on Saturday."

"That just means our next plan has to work," Brooke said, thinking of Haley. "So let's brainstorm."

Paige and Livi still looked discouraged, but Hannah nodded. "She's right, guys," she said, setting her jaw. "Morgan might not think this place is worth fighting for, but I do."

Paige ran her fingers through Foxy's silky mane. "But without Morgan . . ."

"Without Morgan, Robin has too much to do on her own," Brooke said, thinking out loud. "And if we can't get Morgan to come back, we need to figure out a way to replace her so Robin's not overworked anymore."

Livi glanced at her over Foxy's back, her hazel eyes skeptical. "Replace Robin's daughter? How are we supposed to do that?"

"No, she's right." Hannah sounded thoughtful. "I mean, yeah, I'm sure Robin misses working alongside her daughter and all that. But she mostly just needs more help to keep the place running—that's what she told Preston, remember?"

"I guess." Paige shrugged. "But she said she doesn't have enough money to pay more help."

"Right," Brooke said, giving Gideon a pat as he shoved his nose over the fence, looking for more treats. "So we need to figure out a way to help her get the money. Somehow."

"I know!" Livi brightened. "I saw this movie on TV

once where a bunch of kids had a big yard sale to raise money to save their cheerleading squad or something. They all donated some of their stuff and got other people to donate too."

"Ooh! I could donate some of my clothes I don't wear anymore," Paige said.

"Um, guys?" Brooke spoke up. "I'm not sure we have time to set up a yard sale. Besides, hardly anyone lives around here—who's going to come buy your stuff?"

"Oh. I guess you're right," Hannah said. "Okay, then how about a horse show? Robin does a great job with our end-of-camp show every year."

"You're right!" Livi sounded excited again. "And a lot of the big horse shows are charity events—you know, trying to raise money for local hospitals or whatever."

"And people come from miles around to go to those." Paige straightened Foxy's mane. "I'm sure lots of people would come. We can even ride in it ourselves! It'll be fun!"

Brooke bit her lip. She hated to keep shooting down their ideas, but she was still keeping Haley's advice in mind. She didn't want them to waste time on impractical ideas.

"That does sound fun," she said carefully. "But it also sounds like a ton of work. Besides, the thing is, Robin needs money to pay workers all year round. One event won't be enough."

She was starting to wonder if the other girls really even understood the problem. Their families were all wealthy—they'd probably never had to worry about how to afford anything they wanted in their whole lives.

Hannah frowned, looking slightly annoyed. "Okay, then how about we try to find Robin more boarders?" she said. "That way she'll have more money all year round."

This time Paige was the one to shoot down the idea. "But more boarders means more work, and she's already got too much to do," she said. "Besides, if she fills up all her stalls there won't be room for us. Or for her training horses either."

"Yeah. And she loves training." Livi sighed, picking at a splinter on the fence. "I don't know, guys. Don't you think if there was an easy way to do this, Robin already would've thought of it?"

"Not necessarily," Paige said. "My stepdad's always

saying most people don't know anything about running a successful business."

Livi rolled her eyes. "Whatever. I'm just saying, if Robin wanted more boarders or whatever, she'd already be trying to get them, right?"

"Maybe not, if she's too busy running the farm to think about it," Hannah said.

Brooke stroked Foxy's nose and listened to the others argue, feeling as if there was something they were missing. There had to be a way to do this. Maybe she needed to think more like her parents. Her stepfather prided himself on always being able to close a sale. And her mother liked to say that when a deal was going south, that was the time to get creative. . . .

"I've got it!" Brooke blurted out so suddenly that Foxy jumped and even Gideon turned to stare at her with his big sleepy eyes. "Development rights!"

"Huh?" Livi blinked at her.

"My mom's a real estate agent," Brooke explained. "A couple of months ago, she had a client who lost his job and needed money. He had a huge property but didn't want to sell it, so instead Mom worked out a deal where he just sold the development rights—it's kind of complicated, and to be honest, I didn't pay that much attention when she talked about it, but basically I think someone paid him not to ever subdivide his land. If he sells it, it has to go in one big piece, and it can't ever have lots more houses built on it or whatever."

Paige's eyes lit up. "Robin could totally do that!" she cried, waving a hand around so vigorously that Foxy took a step away, eyeing her with suspicion. "She has a large property!"

"Exactly." Brooke grinned at her.

Hannah was frowning. "Wait, but who would want to pay for something like that?"

"Well . . ." Brooke thought back, trying to recall the details of her mother's boring dinner-table talk. "I'm pretty sure it was a conservation group or something like that? Like, someone who wants to keep more large properties and open space and stuff in our town."

"Okay." Hannah still sounded unconvinced. "But how do we find a group like that before next weekend?"

Brooke's shoulders slumped. She hadn't thought that far ahead. "I don't know," she said.

"Could you call your mom?" Paige suggested. "Maybe she could hook you up with the same group."

"I don't think that would work," Brooke said. "I'm pretty sure that group was local. Maybe we could ask around to see if there's a group like that here, though."

"Ask who?" Hannah said. "We can't ask Robin or she'll know we're onto her."

"What about the boarders?" Paige suggested.

"They'd probably tell Robin." Livi shrugged. "And we don't really know anyone else, except maybe that weird old lady Brooke met."

"Yeah." Hannah snorted. "And she doesn't exactly look like the type who'd know lots of rich people with money to spend on other people's land. I mean, did you see that sweater she was wearing? It looked like it was probably knitted by, like, Betsy Ross or someone."

Livi giggled. "Yeah."

Brooke winced. Did the other girls even know how they sounded sometimes? Maybe this was pointless. How could a bunch of wealthy girls even understand this kind of problem?

Then she gasped as she realized she'd just hit on the solution. "Your parents!" she blurted out. "That's who we should ask!"

"Our parents?" Paige echoed. Hannah and Livi just looked confused.

"Uh-huh. Your parents probably all have, like, investments and stuff, right?" Brooke said.

Hannah shrugged. "Sure, I guess. Why?"

"Why not see if they want to invest in some real estate?" Brooke grinned. "Specifically, *this* real estate. Maybe one of them will want to buy Robin's development rights!"

"Or *all* of them." Hannah's dark eyes were thoughtful as she rubbed Gideon's nose. "We could get them to chip in, like one of the investment groups my dad does contracts for."

Paige gasped. "Genius!" she cried. "That way we'd all be, like, part owners of Pocomoke Stables!"

"Cool," Livi said. "Do you think Robin would give us a discount on camp?"

Hannah shot her an annoyed look. "*So* not the point, Livi."

"No, this could really work, guys." Paige looked excited.

"We should get the olders to talk to their families too."

"Good idea." Brooke smiled at her. "The more the merrier, right?"

"Right." Paige grinned back. "Let's all try to get in touch with our parents as soon as we can, okay?"

Hannah pulled out her phone. "I'm sure mine have already left for their usual Saturday night dinner party right now. But I'll text them to call me first thing tomorrow."

"Well, it's unanimous." Paige collapsed at the dinner table on Sunday evening, glancing at Robin and Preston to make sure they weren't close enough to hear her. "My parents finally got back to me."

The bite of bread Brooke had just taken suddenly tasted like dirt in her mouth. "No go, huh?" she said.

Paige just shook her head and reached for the water pitcher.

"I can't believe it." Livi slumped in her chair. "This totally should have worked!"

Brooke winced as Preston let out a bark of laughter from the other end of the table. She didn't know what he and

Robin were talking about, but Preston had been in a good mood all afternoon. That couldn't be a good sign, especially now that the girls' plan had officially failed. Hannah, Livi, and Paige had contacted their parents about investing in Pocomoke Stables. So had most of the older campers. But none of the parents were willing to consider the idea.

Brooke was still thinking about it as the girls went to check on their horses after dinner. As they entered the barn, Livi reached over and gave Brooke's arm a squeeze.

"Don't look so sad, Brooke," she said. "It was worth a shot, right?"

"I guess." Brooke glanced around the tidy room at the contented horses snoozing or eating hay in their stalls. It was hard to believe all this would soon be gone.

"No, she's right, Brooke," Paige agreed. "It's amazing how hard you're trying to save this place."

"Yeah." Livi giggled. "No wonder you convinced your parents to take you to the pony penning to get Foxy! You totally know how to get stuff done."

Hannah nodded. "Like the way you and your friends got your Pony Post website up and running," she said, wandering over to pat a horse that was hanging its head out over the stall door. "Not everyone could do something like that. Especially someone our age."

"Yay, Brooke!" Livi cheered, pumping her fist. "She makes things happen!"

Brooke just stared at the three of them, astounded. Did they really see her that way, as someone who got stuff done? She knew plenty of people like that—her parents, her Pony Post friends—but she'd never thought of herself as one of them.

Paige threw an arm around Brooke's shoulders. "Anyway, whatever happens with Robin and the stable, I'm glad you came to Camp Pocomoke this year," she said.

"Me too," Hannah put in. "If not for you, I still wouldn't have tried bareback riding."

Livi smiled at Brooke. "If a miracle happens and Robin decides not to sell after all, I hope you come back next year."

"Definitely!" Paige and Hannah chorused.

Brooke was touched. She didn't have much in common with these girls other than horses. Did they really like her? Maybe that wasn't so strange—after all, she realized she liked all of them. Yes, they were a lot different from her. But so what? Her Pony Post friends were different from her too. That was just part of what made their friendship work so well.

"I don't know about next year," Brooke said, thinking about how much camp cost. What were the chances her stepfather would sell another expensive car at just the right time?

"What do you mean?" Paige sounded disappointed.

Looking at the other girls' faces, Brooke decided it didn't matter. Pocomoke Stables probably wasn't even going to be around next summer, so why not play along? One corner of her mouth twitched up in a half smile.

"I mean, there are only four bunks," she said. "If your friend Lauren comes back, I don't want to end up sleeping on the floor."

Livi laughed. "No way!" she said. "We'll just kick Hannah out to the olders' cabin to make room."

"Hey!" Hannah sounded outraged. "Forget it, I'm not listening to Jenna talk about herself for two weeks straight." She smiled at Brooke. "We'll just make Robin put in an air mattress or something."

"Ooh, dibs on the air mattress!" Livi exclaimed. "That's got to be more comfortable than those bunks."

Brooke laughed. "Maybe we can draw straws for the air mattress."

"See?" Paige hugged her again. "Brooke really does know how to make things work!"

"Yeah. And you know what? I'm not giving up yet." Brooke looked around at the beautiful barn and the sleek, contented horses. "We still have five more days, right? That should be enough time to think up a new plan."

By the time the younger campers gathered in the barn for their Tuesday afternoon riding lesson, they were frantic. "Anything?" Paige demanded as soon as they were all together. "Come on, guys. We have to think of something!"

Brooke just shook her head. They'd spent the past day and a half brainstorming every chance they got. But so far, nobody had come up with a workable plan to save the stable.

Livi looked just as gloomy as Brooke felt. "Maybe we should give up," she said. "I mean, we're just kids. What can we possibly do to—"

She cut herself off as Robin hurried in. "Let's move, people," she said, pulling out her cell phone. "I've got a million things to do today, and we need to stay on schedule. I'll see you in the ring shortly."

"Okay." Hannah shot the other girls a worried glance.

Brooke watched Robin disappear into the barn's small office with her phone pressed to her ear. The stable owner had seemed distracted all day. Was that because she was thinking about the sale? She'd been on her phone a lot—was she working out the details with Preston's friend?

No, Brooke told herself. *Robin told Preston she wouldn't decide until camp was over. We still have time. We just have to think of something that will work!*

A few minutes later the girls were in the ring, warming up their horses. Robin hadn't appeared yet, and nobody else was in sight except a boarder hand-grazing her horse on the other side of the driveway.

"I wonder where Preston is?" Livi said as she rode past Brooke. "I haven't seen him since lunch yesterday."

"Me neither." Brooke nudged Foxy gently with one leg, steering her around a jump.

"I hope he's not in town today, like, preparing the paperwork to make the sale official," Livi said.

Paige heard her and rode closer. "No way," she said. "Robin said she wasn't going to make a decision until Saturday."

Livi shrugged. "Maybe he talked her into deciding sooner."

"Shh!" Brooke nodded toward the gate. "Robin's here."

"All right, girls," Robin said briskly, striding to the center of the ring. "The end-of-camp show is just three days away, and we still have work to do. Let's begin by focusing on lateral work. You could all use some more practice on that."

"Yeah, we definitely want to do our best, since it's probably our last show ever," Livi blurted out. Her eyes immediately went wide, and she took a hand off the reins to cover her mouth. "Oops," she mumbled.

Robin tilted her head to the side. "Last show ever?" she said. "What are you talking about?"

Livi pulled her hand away. "I don't mean it's our last show *ever* ever," she said. "Just the last one here at camp."

"Zip it, Livi," Hannah muttered.

But Robin stepped closer, and Brooke could tell she

was really focusing on them—maybe for the first time all day. "Hang on, is something going on that I should know about?" Robin asked. "Why do you all look so weird?"

All four girls traded a glance. Brooke took a deep breath. "We know you're thinking about selling the farm," she said.

"What?" Robin's eyes widened in shock. "How did you find out?"

"I overheard you talking to Preston last week," Brooke admitted, clutching the reins so tightly that Foxy took a step backward. "It was an accident—I'm sorry."

"You can't sell Pocomoke Stables to some horrible condo builder!" Paige cried.

"Yeah," Hannah agreed. "If you give us a little more time, we can help you come up with a plan. We've been thinking about it nonstop for like the past week, and—"

"I know!" Livi blurted out. "Maybe you could try asking for money on the Internet—I heard that works sometimes."

"Hang on." Robin held up a hand, and the girls fell silent. An odd little smile played over her face. "You can save your breath with the elaborate plans, girls. Because the place is already sold."

◆ CHAPTER ◆ 12

BROOKE'S HEART SANK. "WHAT?" SHE blurted out.

"No!" Livi cried

Hannah shook her head, her expression stormy. "I can't believe it," she muttered. "Seriously, I can't believe this!"

Robin glanced over her shoulder at the driveway. *Is she looking for Preston?* Brooke wondered, feeling sick to her stomach. Her gaze was drawn to the horses in the pasture on the other side of the drive, and her eyes filled with tears. It was such a beautiful, peaceful scene. And soon . . .

At that moment there was the roar of a motor, and then a car came up the driveway. It was a station wagon, so old and decrepit that Brooke couldn't tell what color it had originally been—definitely nothing like Preston's flashy red sports car.

"Aha." Robin smiled. "I think this will answer any questions you might have."

Brooke glanced at the other girls. They all looked mystified.

Then Miss Alice climbed out of the car's passenger seat. She spotted the group in the ring and waved, her cane dangling from her hand as she rushed over. Meanwhile, her nephew jumped out of the driver's side.

"Aunt Alice, wait!" he called. "The ground is so uneven, I don't want you to fall. . . ."

Miss Alice ignored him. She reached the fence and leaned her cane against it. "Sorry I'm late," she told Robin. "My nephew drives like an old lady."

"No worries, you're right on time." Robin smiled at Brooke and the others. "Girls, I'd like to introduce you to the new co-owner of Pocomoke Stables, Miss Alice Foster."

"Co-owner?" Brooke echoed, confused. Visions of Miss Alice and Preston standing side by side, directing a line of bulldozers, flashed through her head.

"That's right." Miss Alice sounded pleased. "Robin was kind enough to sell me a half share in this place. Of course, she's the expert, so she'll continue running it as she sees fit. But I'll be here to get in her way and put my two cents in. It'll give me something to do other than knock around my big old house." She glanced toward the driveway. "Besides, the girls will love helping out around the barn."

Brooke looked that way too. Two teenagers had climbed out of the car by now. One was the girl she'd seen on the beach the first time she'd met Miss Alice. The other was a couple of years younger.

"This place is awesome!" the younger teen exclaimed, rushing over to join Miss Alice by the fence. "Hi, Ms. Montgomery."

"Hello, Nicole." Robin smiled at the girl. "I'm glad you and your sister could finally come over to see the place. Maybe my campers can give you a tour after their lesson." She glanced at Brooke and the others. "Nicole and Natalie did some riding back in California, and they're hoping to start up again."

"Hold on," Hannah said. "Who are they? What's going on? I don't get it."

"Keep up, girl," Miss Alice replied, with a flash of the crankiness Brooke had seen during their first meeting. "I'm buying into the business, and my nephew's daughters are going to learn the value of hard work by helping out in exchange for their riding lessons. It's a good thing all around: keeps the neighborhood safe from development. Helps out a neighbor. Gives me something to do with some extra money I had lying around." She smiled at Brooke. "Meeting Brooke and Foxy reminded me how much I used to love being around horses. And when Brooke mentioned that Robin was considering selling this place . . ."

"Yes." Robin raised an eyebrow at Brooke. "Normally, I'd be annoyed that she shared something like that. But in this case, it worked out for the best."

Brooke ducked her head. "Sorry. I wasn't trying to blab about your business, honest."

"Yes, give her a break," Miss Alice advised Robin. "I scared it out of her. I tend to have that effect on young people."

Natalie, the older teen, had joined her sister by now. "Yeah, you might not want to hang around when new campers show up, Great-Aunt Alice," she teased her with a grin. "You'll scare all Robin's business away!"

Miss Alice snorted. "Teenagers—so disrespectful these days!" But her blue eyes were twinkling as she winked at Brooke.

"Wow." Livi glanced from Miss Alice's ratty sweater to her battered car and back again. "Um, so you're spending all your money to save this place?"

"*All* my money?" Miss Alice snorted again. "Hardly!"

"Miss Alice is one of the wealthiest landowners in the area," Robin informed Livi and the others. "Not that it's any of your business."

Livi looked sheepish, and Brooke felt the same. She never would have guessed that Miss Alice was rich either.

Dan had joined his daughters at the fence by then. "So this is the famous Brooke, huh?" he asked, smiling at her. "Thank you, young lady. I haven't seen Aunt Alice so happy in years. And it's all thanks to you."

"Oh, don't be so dramatic, Daniel." Miss Alice rolled

her eyes. "But you're right, Brooke is the one who made all this happen."

Robin laughed. "Even if she didn't mean to."

"Yay, Brooke!" Livi cheered so loudly that her horse sidestepped, putting his ears back. "It's a good thing you came to camp this year!"

"Yeah," Paige added. "I can't believe how perfectly everything is working out for everyone!"

"Well, almost everyone," Robin put in. "Poor Preston isn't thrilled with this new turn of events, I'm afraid." She shrugged. "I suppose he'll get over it eventually."

Brooke glanced at the other girls. That explained why Preston hadn't been around all day!

Dan checked his watch. "I hate to rush things," he said apologetically. "But I'd really like to get the paperwork moving before the end of the day. Robin, do you have a moment to go over everything?"

"You mean right now?" Robin hesitated, glancing at the girls. "Well, I'm supposed to be teaching this lesson. . . ."

"Go!" Paige cried, dropping her reins and waving her hands at Robin. "We don't mind!"

Robin glanced at the barn. "I could see if Felicia's around; at least she could supervise your ride, or—"

"Seriously!" Hannah exclaimed. "Get out!"

Robin laughed. "Okay, I hear you. I'm going." She ducked under the fence and headed toward the house with Dan and Miss Alice.

"Is your dad a lawyer or something?" Brooke asked Natalie and Nicole, who were still leaning on the fence.

"Uh-huh," Nicole said. "He specializes in real estate law."

Natalie grinned. "Pretty convenient, huh?"

"Yeah." Paige glanced at Brooke. "Just one more thing that worked out just like it was supposed to."

"Except for poor, poor Preston," Hannah added with a smirk.

"Who's Preston?" Natalie asked as Brooke and the others laughed.

Paige shrugged. "Oh, nobody much," she said. "Come help us put our horses away and we'll tell you all about him while we give you that tour of the farm Robin was talking about."

Brooke held her breath as she and Foxy neared the short end of the ring. Using her legs, seat, and hands, Brooke reminded the pony to bend into the turn. Foxy responded perfectly, dropping her head and cantering around in perfect form.

"Okay, girlie," Brooke whispered. "Last line of the course, coming up!"

It was their final course of the show. Their other classes had gone pretty well, but so far this was their best yet. They'd met every jump out of stride, with no awkward moments or bobbled turns.

Foxy's ears pricked as they neared the second-to-last jump, an airy vertical with yellow-and-white-striped poles. For a second the mare slowed, peering at the evergreen boughs piled underneath the jump as filler. But a gentle nudge from Brooke's legs got her moving again. They met the jump at the perfect distance, Foxy folding her legs neatly for takeoff while Brooke shoved her hands forward to give the pony all the freedom she needed to stretch her neck over the jump.

The final jump went just as well. Afterward, Foxy

seemed to know she was finished. She sped up, shaking her head and snorting as she cantered her final circle. Brooke could hear the other campers cheering as she pulled up near the gate.

"Good girl!" she exclaimed, grinning ear to ear as she gave Foxy a pat. "What a good girl!"

"You were amazing, Brooke!" Paige exclaimed as she swung open the gate so Brooke could ride out. "It's hard to believe you and Foxy never jumped a course before you came here."

"Or entered a show." Brooke patted her pony again. "I know—Foxy's incredible."

She glanced back into the ring. Robin had been standing in the middle, judging the classes all day. Miss Alice's nephew Dan had been with her for most of that time, leaving only occasionally to fetch her a snack or a bottle of water. Otherwise, he'd stayed busy handing out ribbons after each class, adjusting the volume on Robin's microphone, or just holding her clipboard and pen. He looked sunburned and happy now as he watched Robin make notes on her judge's card.

"Are you thinking what I'm thinking?" Hannah asked with a smirk, following Brooke's gaze.

"I don't know. What are you thinking?" Brooke asked.

"I know," Livi singsonged. "She's thinking Robin and Dan have been looking awfully chummy the past few days. Especially today."

The thought hadn't really occurred to Brooke until that moment. Miss Alice had been around a lot since the big announcement on Tuesday afternoon, which made sense. Natalie and Nicole, too—they'd come every day.

But now she realized Dan had been there every day too, even though Robin had already signed all the paperwork.

"And you'll notice we haven't seen poor Preston all week, hmm?" Paige added. "Maybe by this time next year, Dan will be living at Pocomoke Stables so Miss Alice can have her house back to herself!"

Brooke smiled at the thought, though she couldn't help feeling a little sad. Whatever happened between Robin and Dan, she'd have to hear about it secondhand. There was no way her stepfather would pay for her to come to camp next summer, and even less of a chance that Brooke could save up enough herself between now and then while also taking care of Foxy as usual.

"What?" Livi asked, peering into Brooke's face. "Why do you look sad all of a sudden?"

Brooke let out a sigh. Why not tell them the truth? They'd find out eventually anyway.

"I'm not sad, I'm happy," she said. "It's just that, well, I probably can't come to camp again next year, and I'm going to miss it. I'll miss all of you guys, too."

"What do you mean, you can't come next year?" Paige looked heartbroken. "You have to!"

"Yeah, it wouldn't be the same without you," Hannah added. "I'll buy the air mattress myself if I have to!"

Livi nodded vigorously. "And Lauren's dying to meet you. I've been texting her all about you."

Brooke shrugged. "The thing is, my family can barely afford to keep Foxy as it is." Two weeks ago, she would have been embarrassed to tell them that. But they were her friends now, and she wanted to be honest with them. "This was a onetime thing after my stepdad sold a fancy car to Lauren's dad, and we just can't afford—"

"Never mind about that, young lady," Miss Alice's voice broke in.

Brooke turned and saw the old lady leaning on her cane just a couple of feet away. "Miss Alice?" she said.

"Sorry to eavesdrop, but you young people talk so loudly these days." Miss Alice stepped closer. "In any case, Brooke, you won't have to worry about how to pay for Camp Pocomoke next summer. After all you did to make this deal happen, the least I can do is sponsor you for as long as you want to keep coming back."

Livi's eyes lit up. "Awesome!"

"Yeah, that's great," Hannah said, and Paige just grinned.

"Are you sure?" Brooke blurted out. "I mean, thank you! But are you sure you want to do that?"

"Absolutely." Miss Alice nodded toward the ring. "Now hush up, all of you chatterboxes. Robin's about to announce the awards."

Brooke was too stunned to say anything else anyway. She was coming back! Suddenly she didn't even care that much about the award ceremony—she'd just won the best prize ever!

But she gathered near the gate with the others, Foxy trailing along at the end of her reins, as Robin named the winners of the last jumping class. Brooke and Foxy came in third, just behind Hannah and one of the olders!

After that, Robin went on to read off a list of special awards. Some were serious, like Best Equitation, which Robin awarded to one of the older campers. Others were humorous—Livi won a ribbon for Most Talkative, and Hannah took the prize for Tallest Horse.

Brooke cheered every time her friends' names were called—Livi also won Best-Groomed Horse, while Paige got a sportsmanship ribbon and one for Best Flatwork, and Hannah was awarded Best Overall Younger Rider. Brooke's friends cheered just as loudly when Brooke won Shortest Horse and Best Bareback Equitation. The two extra ribbons looked jaunty hanging on Foxy's bridle along with the ones they'd earned in their classes.

"And now, one last award," Robin announced. "It might be the most important one of the day, because it shows the recipient is eager to improve herself and her horse." She cleared her throat. "And the ribbon for

Most-Improved Overall Horse and Rider goes to—Brooke and Foxy!"

The place exploded in cheers. Hannah whistled loudly right in Brooke's ear, making her wince and laugh.

"Come on out and accept your trophy, Brooke," Robin called. "You earned it."

As Brooke hurried into the ring, leaving Foxy with Paige, Dan pulled a horse-and-rider-shaped gold trophy out of the ribbon box and held it out. "Congratulations, Brooke," he said with a smile.

"Thanks." Brooke smiled back shyly as she accepted the trophy. She couldn't wait to show it to her family and her Pony Post friends—mostly because she knew she and Foxy really *had* earned it. They'd both learned a lot over the past two weeks, and not just about riding.

Brooke turned and held the trophy over her head like the athletes on TV, which brought more cheering from everyone. For a second she felt sad again as she looked at all her new friends—her bunkmates, Miss Alice and her family, Felicia and Abby, several boarders who'd turned up to watch the show, even the olders—but she shook the feeling off quickly. Why be sad that camp was ending and she wouldn't see them for a while? It just gave her a reason to look forward to *next* summer.

"I know, it's not nearly as fancy as your deluxe stall at Pocomoke Stables, is it?" Brooke smiled as she rubbed her pony's neck. She'd just led Foxy into her little home barn and let her loose. "But it's still home sweet home."

Foxy let out a snort, lifting her head and looking around. Spotting the drafts snoozing in their usual spot under the oak, the pony took off at a trot, calling to them.

Brooke smiled as she watched Foxy go. She missed camp already, but it was good to be home, too.

The house was quiet when she went inside. The whole family had come to pick her up at camp, but they'd already scattered—Brooke's stepfather and the twins to the community pool and Brooke's mother to an open house. But Brooke didn't mind. She'd promised her Pony Post friends she'd check in as soon as possible, and she didn't want to keep them waiting.

She went up to her room and grabbed her laptop. First she checked her e-mail. There were already two messages waiting for her from Livi and one each from Paige and Hannah. Brooke scanned them, smiling at Livi's second one—she'd already tracked down the latest gossip and discovered that Preston was out of the picture for good, and Robin and Dan were going out on their first official date next weekend.

"Awesome," Brooke whispered with a shiver, still amazed how everything had worked out.

Making a mental note to write back to her new friends later, she loaded the Pony Post and scanned the latest entries.

[HALEY] R u home yet B? We want to hear all about it!

[NINA] Ditto! Hope u and Foxy had a smooth ride home!

[MADDIE] Post pics as soon as u can, OK?

Brooke opened a text box and started to type, filling her friends in on the show results and the gossip she'd just learned from Livi's e-mail. She hit send, then sat back in her chair, glancing around her room. Her stepfather had carried in her stuff while she got Foxy settled, and Brooke's suitcase and other things were piled haphazardly just inside the door. But he'd taken the time to set her trophy in a place of honor on top of her bookcase. It looked good, and Brooke was pretty sure she was going to leave it there.

She opened another text box.

> [BROOKE] Almost forgot 1 more thing. We all got up early this a.m. so we'd have time for a trail ride. We decided to ride over to Miss Alice's to say bye & thank her for everything. The other horses don't go trail riding much, so they were kinda spooky at first. lol. But good ol' Foxy just marched along like a pro and showed them how it's done! The other girls were totally impressed. So I guess Foxy & I weren't the only ones who

learned a lot at camp. The others might've learned

a lil something from us too! Isn't that cool?

Just as she hit send again, the doorbell rang. When Brooke ran downstairs and opened the door, Adam was standing there.

"Hey," he said, shoving his hands in his shorts pockets. "Heard you were home. Didn't realize you'd be here so early—I was going to help you get Foxy off the trailer and stuff."

"Oh." Brooke pushed her glasses up her nose, a little surprised to see him. "Um, thanks. But actually, she was fine on the trailer. I got her on and off myself, no problem." She couldn't help thinking again how much she and Foxy had learned at camp. "Anyway, we just got home a little while ago. How's everything been around here?"

He shrugged. "Boring, as usual. So, I heard the fish are biting over at Crooked Creek. Want to go check it out? You can borrow my extra pole if you want."

Brooke smiled. "Yeah, sounds good. Just give me a sec."

She ran back upstairs just long enough to tell her Pony Post friends she'd check in again later. Then she logged off the Internet and headed out of the room again, giving her trophy a pat on the way.

She already missed Camp Pocomoke, and would be counting the days until next summer. Still, it was definitely nice to be home.

• Glossary •

Chincoteague pony: A breed of pony found on Assateague Island, which lies off the coasts of Maryland and Virginia. Chincoteague ponies are sometimes referred to as wild horses, but are more properly called "feral" since they are not native to the island but were brought there by humans sometime many years past. There are several theories about how this might have happened, including the one told in the classic novel *Misty of Chincoteague* by Marguerite Henry. The novel also details the world-famous pony swim and auction that still takes place in the town of Chincoteague to this day.

bareback riding: Riding without a saddle.

crossties: Crossties are used to tie a horse or pony so it will stand in one place for grooming or for other reasons. Crossties consist of two ropes or chains, each attached to a different wall or other sturdy object, with clips on the ends. The two crossties are clipped to the two sides of the horse's halter. As with everything else, horses must be trained to stand quietly and safely in crossties.

curry comb: A grooming tool used to bring dust and dirt to the surface of a horse or pony's coat so it can be brushed off.

draft horse: Heavy horses developed for hard work, such as pulling plows or wagons. Some of the most common draft breeds are the Clydesdale, the Belgian draft, and the Percheron.

filly: A young or baby female horse or pony.

hand: A unit of measurement for horse height. One hand is equivalent to four inches. A pony is an equine under 14.2 hands tall at the withers. Any equine taller than that is a horse.

hoofpick: A grooming tool used to clean a horse's hooves.

leg yielding: A dressage movement in which a horse is asked to move sideways and forward at the same time.

pulling a mane: A method of shortening, thinning, and neatening a horse or pony's mane, in which hairs are pulled out at the root. Most horses and ponies don't mind this; it doesn't hurt them!

stall: An enclosure, usually inside a barn or other building, where an individual horse or pony can be housed.

yearling: A horse or pony that is between one and two years of age.

withers: The ridge between the horse or pony's shoulder bones. This is normally the highest part of the back, and is where a horse or pony's height is measured.

Marguerite Henry's Ponies of Chincoteague

is inspired by the award-winning books by Marguerite Henry, the beloved author of such classic horse stories as *King of the Wind*; *Misty of Chincoteague*; *Justin Morgan Had a Horse*; *Stormy, Misty's Foal*; *Misty's Twilight*; and *Album of Horses*, among many other titles.

Learn more about the world of Marguerite Henry at www.MistyofChincoteague.org.

Don't miss the next book in the series!

Book 3: *Chasing Gold*